Coke Kings 2

Lock Down Publications and Ca$h Presents

Coke Kings 2

A Novel by *T.J. Edwards*

Lock Down Publications
P.O. Box 870494
Mesquite, Tx 75187

Visit our website @
www.lockdownpublications.com

Copyright 2019 T.J. Edwards
Coke Kings 2

First Edition August 2019
Printed in the United States of America

This is a work of fiction. Names, characters, places, and incidents either are products of the author's imagination or are used fictitiously. Any similarity to actual events or locales or persons, living or dead, is entirely coincidental.

Lock Down Publications
Like our page on Facebook: Lock Down Publications @
www.facebook.com/lockdownpublications.ldp
Cover design and layout by: **Dynasty Cover Me**
Book interior design by: **Shawn Walker**
Edited by: **Lashonda Johnson**

Stay Connected with Us!

Text **LOCKDOWN** to 22828 to stay up-to-date with new releases, sneak peaks, contests and more…

Thank you.

Submission Guideline.

Submit the first three chapters of your completed manuscript to ldpsubmissions@gmail.com, subject line: Your book's title. The manuscript must be in a .doc file and sent as an attachment. Document should be in Times New Roman, double spaced and in size 12 font. Also, provide your synopsis and full contact information. If sending multiple submissions, they must each be in a separate email.

Have a story but no way to send it electronically? You can still submit to LDP/Ca$h Presents. Send in the first three chapters, written or typed, of your completed manuscript to:

LDP: Submissions Dept
Po Box 870494
Mesquite, Tx 75187

DO NOT send original manuscript. Must be a duplicate.

Provide your synopsis and a cover letter containing your full contact information.

Thanks for considering LDP and Ca$h Presents.

T.J. Edwards

Chapter 1

Part One Continued

Kammron began beating on the door to Bonkers' apartment. "Yo, open up, Kid. Open the damn door!" He beat some more.

Bonkers grabbed the Tech-9 from under the bed and rushed to put his shorts on. Once they were on, he turned to Yasmin who was looking at him terrified.

"Yo', stay ya ass in here. I don't give a fuck how long I'm in the other room you stay your ass right in here. Do we understand each other?"

She nodded her head. "Baby, what if it's the police? Then what do we do?" she asked nervously.

"Anything they worried about you tell them muthafuckas you don't know shit, and they need to holler at me. You don't try and be a fuckin' hero. You got that?"

"I got that, baby. Can you kiss me before you go in there, though?" She came to her knees and reached out for him.

Kammron started beating so hard on the door some of Bonkers' neighbors stuck their head out of their doors to see what all the ruckus was about. After he mugged them, they slammed their doors back and locked them.

Bonkers finished tonguing Yasmin down, kissed her lips, and licked all over them. "A'ight Boo, chill in here. Matter fact get on the floor in case some shooting starts.

Yasmin dropped to the floor and followed his directives. She couldn't lie to herself and say that she wasn't scared because she was terrified. "Be careful, baby."

Bonkers nodded, stepped into the hallway and closed the door behind him. He came to the side of his front door with the Tech in his hand. "Yo', who the fuck is it beating on my door like you crazy?"

Kammron kicked the door. "Nigga it's me, open this mafucka," he snapped.

Bonkers took the locks off the door. "Fuck you beating on the door like you the Feds for?"

Kammron rushed in with his head lowered. "Damn, nigga, you got me waiting out here all day and shit." He walked into the living room and paced back and forth.

Bonkers could tell that something was wrong with him right away. He locked the door back. "Yo', what the fuck happened, Kid? I can see that shit written all over your face."

"That bitch know, B." Kammron continued to pace. His right hand rested on the back of his neck.

"What, bitch, and what are you talking about that she knows?"

"Shana, she knows I iced, Shelly man. We just had his big thing, and now she just knows man. I fucked up, I'm losing my mind. I don't know what to do. I gotta kill her, right?" He stopped and looked over to Bonkers for confirmation.

Bonkers frowned and balled his fists. "Yo', how and the fuck she find out. Don't tell me you opened that big ass mouth of yours."

Kammron nodded. "That fuckin' Mollie and Percocets don't mix, Bonkers. I been putting that tar up my nose, and I feel so much better. But now this bitch in the wind. She fucked me up, too. Got my neck all fucked up and whatnot. Yo', I'm vexed. I gotta kill her, right?" he asked this again.

Bonkers shook his head. He didn't know what to do or say. "Bruh, damn! So, you just went on running ya big ass mouth cause you was hopped up on a few pills? Fuck type of shit is that? Where she at now?"

"We got into this big fight, then she ran out the door. She kept saying she wasn't gon' say shit about her sister's murder, but I don't know. That gotta be a tough pill to swallow."

Bonkers massaged his temples and took a deep breath. "We burned shorty to the bone. Then beat them bitches to dust. They don't stand a chance at finding her. But you had to open your fucking mouth. Yo', you constantly screwing us over, Kid. What the fuck?" Bunkers slumped on the couch, lost and pissed off.

Yasmin covered her mouth at hearing how both of them had handled Shelly. The story sent chills down her spine. She also couldn't believe Bonkers had been a part of it. She wondered if he had any part in the actual killing. Her and Shelly had been good friends ever since she was nine years old. Her ending sounded tragic. It made Yasmin question everything, including her and Yazzy's safety for the long haul.

"Yo', you already know I didn't mean to, Kid. When have you ever known me to spill the beans about anything?"

"Right the fuck now, nigga. Damn!" Bonkers hopped up. "Yo', we gotta find her like asap. Ain't no telling who she talking, too, or what she finna do with that information. She could be sitting in front of twelve right now as we speak."

Kammron ran his hand over his face. "Damn, man, fuck." He placed his back on the wall. "I fucked up, Bonkers. I fucked all the way up. I shoulda killed her. I shoulda killed her as soon as I let that shit slip out of my mouth."

Yasmin waited patiently with her hand over her mouth to see what Bonkers' response was going to be. She prayed he would tell Kamm that was a bad idea. That Shelly's family had suffered enough. That more murder was not the answer to their problem. Or that he would remind him Shana was pregnant with his child, and taking her life meant he would also be taking the life of their child. She prayed he'd speak in the positive; that if Kammron had killed Shelly, Bonkers' would convince him to turn himself in. Oh, how she prayed for any of these desired responses. She stood up and opened the door just a tad so she could hear better.

"Yo', that is your mess to clean up. I can't tell you what to do, but you already know they gon' lace your ass over her murder, Kid. On the other hand, Shana got your seed. You whack her, you bodying your shorty, too. Like I said I can't micromanage what you do, but whatever we finna do we gotta get a move on like, right now."

"I gotta kill that bitch, B, it's the only way. If Stacie, finds out I killed her daughter not only would she never forgive me, she'll have them put me under the jail. I can't stomach that, both of them might have to go."

Yasmin was listening so hard she slipped and fell in the hallway. "Aw shit!" she hollered.

Kammron upped two Glocks and rushed down the hall. He pointed both of them at Yasmin. "Yo', this bitch was eaves-dropping the whole time. Hell, nall, Kid. That's one too many witnesses."

Yasmin held her hands in the air. "Baby, come get yo crazy ass friend!"

Bonkers sprinted down the hallway. "Kammron, what the fuck is you doing, Kid? Take them guns off her." He upped the Tech and aimed it down the hall at Kammron's back. "Kammron don't!"

Kammron shook his head and cocked the hammers. "Nall, fuck that, this Bitch getting in between us anyway. If we smoking, Shana, then she gotta go, too. We gotta get this money. Fuck these hoes. It's always been us, Dunn, until this bitch came along." His finger slipped around the triggers, then he was pulling them both back.

Bonkers ran full speed and tackled Kammron from behind just as the guns went off barking inside of Kammron's hands. *Bocka! Bocka! Bocka! Bocka!* The bullets tore up the wall, leaving big chunks inside of them. Plaster wafted into the air and created a big cloud of white smoke.

Yasmin screamed at the top of her lungs, and fell to her knees, covering her head. *"Please-please-please don't kill me!"*

Kammron and Bonkers fell to the floor with Bonkers winding up on top. Kammron tried as hard as he could to buck his right-hand man off him. But he felt weak and helpless. The tireless nights of no sleep were finally catching up with him. He yanked his wrist away from Bonkers and tried to aim his gun.

"Nigga, get the fuck out of the way and quit trying to save this bitch. She gotta go, she heard everything." He aimed and got ready to fire.

Bonkers held his wrist to the carpet. "Kamm, chill nigga. That's my daughter's mother. I can't let you buss her brain like that, Son. Trust me, she ain't gon' say shit."

He wiggled and tried to force Bonkers up off him. "Nigga, get yo' ass off me so I can smoke this bitch. I ain't finna let her be the end of me. Fuck that!"

He tried one more time unsuccessfully to get a clear line of her.

Bonkers slammed his wrists as hard as he could into the floor. Both guns went sliding across the carpet. "Yasmin, get yo' ass up out of here. Go into my room and lock the door. Don't come out until I tell you too. Hurry up!"

Yasmin slowly made it to her feet. She used the wall for leverage, then she was up and making her way down the hall-way. She rushed into the bedroom, slammed the door loudly and dropped to the floor crying her heart out.

Kammron was vexed, he pushed Bonkers as hard as he could, and jumped up. He rushed and grabbed his guns off the floor. "You, stupid ass nigga. Yo', don't tell me this bitch got yo' head all fucked up and shit Kid? Don't tell me you about to turn on me, too!" His temper began to rise higher and higher. His heart pounded in his chest.

Bonkers held his Tech on the side of him. "Yo', you wilding, Kid. I'd never turn on you for nobody. But you fuckin' up, right now. We can't just go around killing everybody because we think they gon' be on bullshit. We been knowing Yasmin all our lives, and we ain't never heard about her being no fuckin' snitch."

"Nigga, that bitch left Harlem! We don't know what the fuck she did where she was just at. All we know she coulda been ran out of the city because she got down on somebody. So, look, I don't give a fuck what you talking about, or what you're thinking. That bitch done heard what took place with us. I can't let that shit ride, Bonkers. You gotta let me do my thing." He made his way in the direction of the bedroom.

Bonkers rushed and blocked his path. "I can't let you do that, Kammron. Nigga, I love you. You my nigga and all that shit, but that's the mother of my daughter, right there. I gotta protect her and give her more than the benefit of the doubt that she gon' keep shit one hunnit. You let me take care of her, it's as simple as that."

Kammron flared his nostrils, took two steps forward and planted his forehead against Bonkers'. "You think I'm finna risk my life on a bitch just cause you got a baby by her?" He sucked his teeth. "Nigga, this is Harlem. We ain't supposed to trust a soul walking this green earth, especially not a bitch under no circumstances." He took a deep breath, tried to calm down and ran his hand over his deep waves. "Now I'ma tell you again, let me handle my bidness. You know how this shit go."

Bonkers refused to make eye contact with him. He was feeling soft, like a sucka—a simp. He'd never chosen a woman over Kammron in their entire lives. Even though he knew he was doing the right thing it still felt weird to him.

"Not this time, Kamm. I can't let you splash my daughter's mother. Fuck that, that shit ain't happening."

Kammron's eyes got big, then lowered into slits. His heart felt like it was being split in two. "Okay, then, that's how you wanna play shit. Cool, protect that bitch then. It's good, word to Kathy." He tucked his guns. "Yo', if I find out you leaked any of this shit to anybody, Yasmin, I'm coming fa ya ass ma'! Word to Jehovah, man." He bumped Bonkers out of the way and left the house, slamming the door so hard the pictures in the living room fell off of the wall.

As soon as the door closed Bonkers lowered his head and sighed. He was praying this event didn't cause him and Kammron to become enemies. They had been best friends ever since they were toddlers. He was having a hard time gathering himself.

Yasmin peeked her head out the door and looked down the hallway. She saw Bonkers standing in the middle of the floor with his head down. He shook it from left to right and appeared to be mumbling to himself.

"Baby, is it good?" she whispered.

Bonkers heard her but ignored her. He felt lost and angry. He closed and locked the front door. Then sat on the couch and placed his Tech on his lap.

Yasmin, tiptoed down the hallway, stepping past the fallen pictures, and areas of the carpet that were covered with drywall from the bullets. "Daddy, are you, okay?" she asked extremely timid.

Bonkers pulled his nose and sniffed hard. He was in need of a fix. He could feel a severe migraine threatening to take over him. "Yo', I told you to keep ya ass in there until I called you. You're so fuckin' hardheaded," he snapped.

Yasmin paused in place and snapped her head backward. "Yo', don't tell me you're mad at me for this shit. I didn't do anything wrong, he tried to kill me," her voice began to crack.

Bonkers kept his head lowered. "Yo', you had no bidness eavesdropping so hard it made you fall into the hallway. Had he not heard you, you would have never been under the gun. The rules of Harlem says he was supposed to kill you asap. I made him break those rules. Now I gotta pay for this shit." He hopped up with the Tech in his hand and faced her. "Yo', you can't say shit to nobody about what you heard. I mean not even ya moms. You understand that?"

She nodded. "That ain't my bidness, Bonkers. I wouldn't ever say anything, to begin with. I'm bred in Harlem just like y'all are. The men ain't no tougher than the women here. Dang y'all need to give us some credit." She rolled her eyes and crossed her arms.

Bonkers casually stepped forward and took a hold of her neck with lightning speed. He slammed her into the wall and placed his face against hers. "Yo', because of me you still got breath in your lungs, but this shit ain't a game. You open them mafuckin' lips and I'ma be forced to become a single parent. Now, I love you, and I'm fuckin' wit' you the long way, but I'll murder yo ass dead if you utter a peep. You get that?"

"Yes," she croaked, as she swallowed, and a tear dropped from her eye.

Bonkers released her. "Take yo ass back in that room for a li'l while, I need to clear my head." He grabbed her arm and led her a bit of the way, before pushing her in the direction of the room.

Not only was Yasmin's feelings hurt, but she had officially become afraid of both Bonkers and Kammron. She knew she needed to come up with a plan so she could get rid of both of them. Her and Yazzy's lives depended on it.

"A'ight, Bonkers, this how you wanna play shit, right?" she whispered to herself. "A'ight, we gon' see then." She entered the room, closed the door and sat on the bed plotting with hatred in her heart for both of them.

T.J. Edwards

Chapter 2

Two weeks had passed, and there had been no mention of Shelly's murder. Kammron neglected to reach out to Shana to find out what she was thinking. He felt it was common sense. Shelly was her older sister. He was responsible for her murder, and upon her finding out about it he'd tried to kill her as well until she'd escaped him.

Kammron had remained cooped up in the apartment for the entire two weeks ordering take out. After two weeks of the same ol' same ol' he was finally ready to get out of the house. Jimmy had hit him up a few hours prior and told him he wanted to meet up with him and Bonkers, he had a surprise for them. A surprise that was guaranteed to make them happy. All Kammron could think about was money as he stepped from the shower and dried his body with a bath towel. He stepped to the mirror and smiled at his reflection. His caramel face looked a bit slimmer, probably because he had a habit of going two days at a time with no food because of his extreme depression. His brown eyes still popped, his waves was beginning to curl up.

'*It's time for a haircut,*' he thought.

He finished drying his body, and slipped into a pair of Polo boxers, just as Stacie started pounding on the front door. By the time Kammron pulled the door open, Stacie had been standing at his door for two minutes. He pulled her inside by her wrists, then looked both ways down the hallway for police, or anything out of the ordinary. After not seeing anything unusual, he closed the door and locked it.

Stacie stood before him a nervous wreck. "Kammron, I'm freaking out, baby. Please tell me you've heard from Shana these last few days?" She was hoping against hope he had.

Kammron was lost. "What?"

Stacie's hope died immediately. "Damn, your response just said everything. You mean to tell me you haven't heard from my daughter either?"

Kammron shook his head. "Me and her ain't rocked in two weeks. I thought she was just taking some time away from me. Maybe she laying low somewhere trying to get her mind right."

Stacie took a seat on the couch. Her sundress rose on her thick thighs and revealed the underside of her thighs. Slight traces of her cellulite was visible. Stacie was strapped, built like a Harlem Goddess. She crossed her thighs and revealed even more of her skin. Stacie was the mother of Shana, Shana was Kammron's baby mother.

Stacie placed her face in her hands. "Baby, I just don't understand what's going on with these girls. First, Shelly goes missing, and now Shana. I mean I know Harlem is a hard place to live, but why are my girls running away and not telling me where they are going? Don't they know that will eventually drive me crazy?"

Kammron slid on the couch beside her and wrapped his arm around her shoulder. The scent of her perfume drifted up his nose. He looked down at her thick thighs, and his mother issues started getting the better of him.

He placed a hand on her thigh. "Mama that's the problem. You gotta quit stressing so much on what they are doing and worry about yourself. Maybe I need to take you out and spend some money on you or something." He kissed her neck and sucked on it loudly.

Stacie moaned and tried to push him away. "Gon' Kammron, I didn't come over her for that. I just thought you knew where my baby was." She extended her arms.

Kammron rubbed all over her caramel thighs and dropped his head between her legs. He forced them apart and felt all around her middle. Her panties felt hot and packed with pussy. This caused his dick to rise. Once again, she was driving him crazy unintentionally.

He licked her neck. "Mama, I gotta have you."

Stacie moaned, as she felt his fingers slip through the leg holes of her panties and play over her naked sex lips. He opened them and slipped a finger into her hot, moist hole.

She jerked into his finger and threw her head back. "Kammron, Son-unnhhh. What are you doing? Please stop," she groaned. "I said we couldn't do this no more."

Stacie's pleas fell on deaf ears. Kammron fingered her with blazing speed, watching his digits go in and out of his bm's mother's pussy. It drove him crazy.

"I'm finna make you cum, Mama. I'm finna make you cum. That's all you need to do, cum fa me!" He fingered her faster, and harder.

Stacie tried to fight him off again, but her thighs opened widely on their own accord. She placed her right foot on the couch, arched her back and bussed her pussy wide open for him. "Kammron! Kammron! Uhhhhhhhh, shit baby-Mama finna—ooo!" Her tongue licked over her lips as she came hard. "Ahhhhh!"

He kneeled on the floor, pushed her knees to her chest, ripped her panties from her body, and licked up and down her slit loudly, sucking on her clitoris, and running his fingers in and out of her.

"I want some of this pussy, I want some of his pussy, mama!"

"Nooo, baby—no!" Stacie groaned leaking on to his fingers.

She allowed him to lick up and down her crease for a full minute, relishing in the way his tongue played over her clitoris. The way his lips sucked and slurped.

She quivered and felt her next climax fast approaching. "No! No!" She bucked. "Nooooooo baby!" She came hard and threw her head back.

Kammron's fingers were dripping in her fluids now. He pulled them out shiny, and greasy, sucked them into his mouth, and looked over her opening. The lips were puffy and engorged from her sexual cravings. Just as she spread her thighs further apart, she closed them right back together, brought her feet up, and kicked out at him catching him in the shoulder. He flew backward.

She hopped up. "I said no!" She picked her discarded panties from the floor, bending over and exposing her juicy pussy to him. A trail of juice leaked right out of the center of her crease and slid down her thighs. This made Kammron's dick jump in his pants. His head was now throbbing against his stomach, sticky with precum, and she hadn't even touched him. Stacie rushed to the front door and began turning the locks.

Kammron made it to his feet and met her there. He grabbed her by the hair and threw her backward. He locked the door back and turned to face her.

"Where the fuck you think you going, Ma?" His dick was poking through the opening of his Polo boxers, it jumped in the air.

Stacie looked down at it and felt a tingle permeate through her kitty. "Baby, please, no. I don't wanna do this. I got too much on my mind, right now. Besides I need you emotionally. I feel like I'm losing my mind," she whimpered, never once taking her eyes off of his pipe.

Kammron couldn't think about nothing but fuckin' her thick ass. He zoomed in to the way her nipples were poking through her top. He could make out both areolas. They were threatening to poke a hole in the fabric.

He made his way over to her. "Yo, mama, I'm saying, I need you too, right now. Why we can't be here for each other?" He closed the distance between them quickly.

Just as Stacie turned to run, he caught her and forced her to the wall with her back to him. He took his hard dick and smashed it into her crack from the back. The heat from his piece slid up and down her crease. He bit into the back of her neck, causing her to groan. His hips humped forward finding a space between her thick thighs. Her fat ass was all in his lap.

"I want some of this pussy, Ma. Damn, I'm fienin' for it." He humped harder.

Stacie moaned and tried to push back into him to get him off of her, but he added more strength. He kicked her feet apart and slightly bent her over. She felt his hand come between her thighs. He rubbed her slit, two fingers entered into her body, he started finger fucking her at blazing speed, then he removed them. She could hear him licking all over them, while his big head slid into her slit, and eased into her cat. She couldn't help but moan as he invaded her box, stretching her with each inch he added.

Kammron began to shake, her heat swallowed him. She was dripping wet, all of the fantasies he'd had as a little boy began to come back to the forefront. He slammed his dick all the way home, pulled out, and slammed it home again.

"Uhh, Baby, Kammron! Dis ain't right—it ain't right. Please," she whimpered.

He pulled her back a few paces from the wall so he could bend her over. Then he got back into position and began working his dick in and out of her heat. Watching his width spread her as he ran in and out of her like a battering ram.

"Ma-Ma-Ma—fuck-this pussy. Uhhhh-damn, Ma. You so thick-you so thick! You can't blame me. Uhhh, fuck you can't blame me!" He held her hips and fucked her faster, and harder, stroking her like an animal.

Stacie closed her eyes and held the wall. She could feel him reaching deep into her womb. Her ass jiggled every time he slammed into her. All sorts of forbidden thoughts ran through her mind. She knew what they were doing was wrong, after all, he was her daughter's baby father, and she'd practically raised him. As bad as the reality of all that was, she couldn't deny the tremors that went through her body. The fact that he wanted her so bad, that he was willing to take it boosted her self-esteem. Made her feel wanted, for her the feeling was bittersweet.

She bounced back into his lap. "Kammron—oooo!"

Kammron smacked that ass hard, he couldn't help watching his dick go in and out of her. He thought about all of the times he'd been over her house when he was just a young teen, and she'd be walking around in her bra, and a pair of small panties all in her butt. Or her red silk gown that was basically transparent. Her big booty had a tendency of swallowing it, and she loved to be all hugged up with him back then. Calling him her son, and saying how much she loved him, not knowing his dick was harder than calculus. He growled and remembered those images, fucking her harder.

"This my pussy, it's my pussy, Mama!" He forced her ass to crash into his lap again and again.

Her pussy queefed, slurped, oozed, and sucked his pipe like a hungry mouth. Stacie's titties bounced up and down in her dress. She felt him take hold of them, and that was too much.

She came screaming, "We're so wrong, Kammron! Uhhhhh, we so wrong!"

Kammron fucked hard for ten more strokes and came in thick jets. Splashing her womb over and over. "Ma-Ma, uhhh—shit!"

Stacie felt him cumming in her, and leaned forward, reached behind her and pulled his dick out of her, but not before he'd cum. She pulled him out and a few strings landed on the back of her chubby ass cheeks.

"No baby, you gon' fuck around and get me pregnant, too. Don't cum in me, that's too much." She dropped to her knees and held his dick while she looked up at him. "You bogus anyway, I can't stand you."

Kammron's piece jumped up and downs and leaked his baby makers. "Yo', later for that shit. Gon' head and clean the God up. Ya baby need you." He grabbed a hand full of her hair. "Suck this mafucka, word up."

Stacie ain't have to be told twice. She sucked him into her mouth and licked away the semen. She swallowed it and continued to slurp away. She couldn't believe Kammron, couldn't believe what he was making her do. She felt so powerless, so angry, so sexually attracted to him, and it was driving her crazy. Her head speared from back to forward in his lap, over and over. The saltiness of his semen only added to her arousal. In a matter of seconds, he stood fully erect.

Kammron took a step back, his piece popped out of her mouth. He stroked his monster. "Yo', I gotta hit that shit some more."

Stacie felt tingles as she started to get up. "Kammron, baby, I gotta go. I gotta!" Before she could get up, he was on her.

They fell to the ground with him between her legs. He lined himself up and forced her knees to her chest. His head slid in, then he was pumping her at full speed, fuckin' hard, ignoring her whimpers that were so sexy to him.

Stacie's mouth was wide open, moaning, and groaning. She felt like she was being split in two as he pounded away and beat her G spot. She could feel her cream sliding down into her ass crack. Kammron sucked on her neck, and fucked her hard for the next thirty minutes, nonstop. By the time he finished she'd cum so much she fell asleep right there on the living room floor.

****

Four hours later, Kammron was the first to rise. He yawned and stretched his arms over his head. His body was calling out for the heroin. He felt chills, sweat peppered along the right side of his forehead. He climbed out of the bed and dug through his top drawer until he located the poison. He glanced over at Stacie and saw she was still sleeping. He jogged to the living room so he could get right. When Stacie came out of the bedroom room ten minutes later, she found Kammron with his head bent sideways, tooting a hefty line of Tar. She stood and looked him over for ten full minutes.

Then stepped into the living room. "You know you wasn't right boy. It's way too much stuff going on for you and I to be doing what we just did. It's not decent."

Kammron looked up and brushed his nose off. He was so high she was a tad blurry to him. "Ma shut all that noise and shit up. The God wanted some of that pussy, and that's what I got. It's over and done wit' now so move on and quit dwelling." He closed his eyes and leaned to the side. He dozed for fifteen seconds and opened his eyes wide. "Bring yo ass over here and sit on my lap," he ordered.

Stacie held her ground. "I can't do that, Kammron. I shouldn't have done it this time. I was bogus. My daughters are missing. I don't know where they are. My mind just isn't right. I'm so vulnerable, baby."

Kammron held out his hand. "Bring yo ass over here, Ma."

She shook her head. "No, I can't be here, right now. I shouldn't have done that." She opened the front door and ran out of it with tears running down her cheek. She made it halfway down the stairs when Kammron hollered.

"Close my muthafuckin' door then!"

She rushed back up the stairs and closed it shut. Then fled from the building feeling like she was ready to break down.

Kammron sat back in the couch and licked his dry lips. "New York about to see a whole new side of me," He mumbled. "It's time to bring this Harlem world shit to the forefront." He cleared his throat. "No more mercy, I'm killing niggas on sight. I want the streets, I gotta have the slums. That nigga Bonkers wanna trade on me for a bitch." He dozed off for five seconds and jolted away. "He can get it, too. Killing niggas, getting rich. I'm Killa, Kamm, Harlem world." He leaned all the way over and dozed off. The drug took its full effect on his system.

T.J. Edwards

Chapter 3

Bonkers popped the cork on the bottle of Moët, and tilted the bottle up, taking huge gulps of it. He burped, and wiped his mouth, then stepped into the living room where two long tables were set up. The middle of the tables was covered with North Korean Tar. Seated around the tables were young hustlers from Harlem ranging from ages twelve to twenty. Bonkers placed four kilos of North Korean on the table and ordered his workers to first aluminum foil the dope, then drop it into mini sandwich bags.

He had smaller ones that would be sold for five dollars, slightly larger new that would go for ten, and the red packs for twenty. He nodded his head, as the operation looked to be flowing smoothly. Jimmy promised to make sure they were eating within two months after they pulled the Ohio hits, and true to his word they were headed along that path. He took another swallow of the Moet and walked to the back of the house, down the back steps that led to the basement.

Kammron and his crew of hustlers, both male, and female were down there bagging up five keys of coke, also imported from North Korea. Kammron looked up and saw Bonkers scoot away from the table and take off his latex gloves. The basement was illuminated by a red, light bulb. The light reflected off his face. He stepped to Bonkers and gave him half of hug.

"Yo', what the deal, God?"

Bonkers cuffed the back of his head as he gave him half of hug. "Nothin', Kid, I just came down here to make sure you were good." He looked past his shoulder and saw Kammron's workers seemed to have a steady flow.

One side of the table chopped at the dope, broke it into chunks, weighed it, and slid it across the table where it was bagged, then dropped into a big Ziploc bag. Kammron had all of his workers naked. He called himself a true Harlem hustler like Nicky Barnes, and Reginae, both Harlem legends.

"Yo', I got this shit under control, Dunn. I would be up there fuckin' wit that heroin, but I ain't got the willpower. The more I see that shit the more I want it. I'm days away from banging it, Kid, word to, Kathy." He sniffed, wiped his nose and looked over his shoulder at the table of workers. "Now this coke shit, I can run this shit all day and never get tired or tempted. I could never get hip to that coke shit. I'm a downer type nigga."

Bonkers continued to watch his workers move. He liked their flow. He nodded. "Yo', as long as you know your strengths kid. Anyway, it goes we finna spend all this shit together. This is our money. This how Jimmy pay us, and it's good. I got three hundred thousand worth of work upstairs. You got three hundred thousand worth of work down here. That's six hundred thousand altogether. We are looking at a take-home of two hundred gees a piece, and we'll put two hundred thousand back into the business. Jimmy got us hitting locks all over the country, every time we do, he says, he gon' hit us with a heavy load of brown and white. All we gotta do is make these numbers add up, and put Harlem on our back, Kid, become legends."

Kammron nodded in agreement. He was imagining having his face on a few billboards in Harlem. "Yo', it's mad starving niggas in Uptown. I'm trying to feed our people and put the youth to work. Ya, feel me? Bitches and all. Money ain't got no gender." He eyed the thighs of one of the strapped redbones that he'd picked up from a hundred fortieth and Lennox.

He wasn't sure of her situation, but he was going to make it his bidness to get her li'l' young ass into bed real soon. He saw she was thicker than a peanut butter choke sandwich and fine as imported silk.

Bonkers poked his finger into the hole of his bulletproof vest and scratched his chest. "Yo', all I care about is that we get this money and go harder than anybody that has ever done it before. Yo', already know I'm riding wit' you until the end my nigga. We most definitely in this shit together. Word to, Janine." They embraced again, and Bonkers' phone vibrated. He looked at the face and saw it was a message from Yasmin telling him she was ready to be picked up. "Yo', hold down the fort while I go snatch up, Yasmin. I'll be right back."

At the utterance of Yasmin's name, Kammron cringed. He didn't like her, he didn't know why, but he didn't. He tried his best to mask his true feelings. Though the conniving part of him was already trying to come up with a plan to get rid of her for good. He hugged Bonkers tighter.

"Yo', gon' head and snatch Wifey up. Tell her I send my regard. When I'ma see my niece?"

Bonkers laughed. "Yo', hopefully soon, Kid. Her mama still reeling about the gat situation, but it's all good. Let her li'l' ass calm down, then we'll see what it do after that. Cool?"

Kammron smiled weakly and had a vision of blowing Yasmin's head off. "Sound good to me. I'll fuck wit' you in a minute Dunn. Love you, fool." Kammron turned his back to him and frowned.

Bonkers jogged up the stairs and stopped midway up them. "Yo', Killa?"

Kammron turned around and put a slight smile on his face. "What's good?"

"Yo', let's step out tonight a something. You wanna fuck wit' a strip club? They got this new joint over on Broadway, right in the heart of Harlem. Supposed to be some of the baddest bitches in the city dancing there."

Kammron imagined what it would feel like to be in a new strip club that was in the heart of Harlem and laughed. "Yo', we'll probably know and have fucked every bitch up in there. I don't know about that, Son, let's play that shit by ear."

Bonkers held his chin and laughed at Kammron's thoughts. "Yo', you might be right. Well, we should do something. Just hit me up."

Kammron eyed the red bone again. "Yo', I'm definitely gon' be getting into something tonight, so we'll see. Now gon' nigga, damn."

****

Bonkers tapped the horn of his Porsche truck and sat back in his seat. He nodded his head to the music blaring out of his speakers. The sun was just fading behind the clouds. The weather was hot and muggy. It was late August, and still, there had been no sign of Fall. Yasmin came out of the hair and nail salon that Bonkers had helped her to cop for herself. After a hard day's work, all she wanted to do was lay back and cuddle with her man. She felt like having her booty rubbed on.

She opened the door to the truck and climbed in. "Hey, Boo." She leaned over and kissed his lips.

Bonkers returned her affections and sat back in his seat. "How was work, Goddess?" He pulled away from the curb.

She sighed. "It's good, but I'ma need a li'l more help obtaining a few more workers. I think five more girls will have that shop running smoothly. I also want to add a massage package. I know plenty of females that would be interested in that." Yasmin had only had the shop for about two months and already she was trying to find ways to maximize her profits. Her vision felt incomplete. She took this shop as a stepping stone that would for sure lead to something better.

"Yasmin you already know, I'm trying to get you right on a positive platform. So, if you think you need more workers then I agree, baby. Just let me know what you want me to do and I got you."

She smiled, she couldn't help falling in love with Bonkers more and more each day. He had become so sweet to her. So, understanding, so supportive. She kept the Shelly thing in the back of her mind so she wouldn't allow herself to fall blindly in love with him, but sometimes living in the moment with Bonkers made her weak.

"Thank you, baby. I'm still trying to figure out all the logistics, but as soon as I do, I'll let you know what I need to progress the business," she sighed again. "I'm hungry." She yawned and covered mouth.

Bonkers continued to cruise. "So, what's good, you wanna go get some Tacos before we pick up, Yazzy, from her after school program?"

Yasmin's stomach growled. "That sounds amazing, baby. How about we go to that joint right down the street from the Apollo amphitheater?"

Bonkers shrugged his shoulders. "Sound good to me." He stopped, made a U-turn in the middle of the street and headed in the opposite direction.

Yasmin frowned and turned his music to *Jhene Aiko*. She wanted to hear *Blue Dream*. As soon as the music began to play, she felt relieved from the pressures of the day. "Damn, I don't know what it is about Jhene, but homegirl just gets me," she began singing along to the music.

Bonkers mugged her. "I don't wanna hear you sing that bitch shit. She ain't even from Harlem, she from L.A. some mafuckin' where."

Yasmin ignored him and continued singing, "I don't care where she from. Dang, you and Kammron is Harlem crazy.

31

J. Edwards

Y'all think everything gotta be from Harlem. If that was the case, we wouldn't be listening to no R&B other than Keith Sweat. Don't get me wrong, he's good, but so are so many other artists."

Bonkers scoffed and put his music back on. "Yo', if it ain't from Harlem, fuck it. That's how I feel." He began nodding his head hard. Then he stopped and cheesed at her.

She rolled her eyes and looked out of the window. "Boy, you so silly." She couldn't deny how fine he was with his dark skin, almond eyes, and naturally curly hair that was shaved and tapered into a Mohawk. He was always dressed to the nines and to her his swag was amazing. "Bonkers when are we going to move out of Harlem?"

He looked her over and kept rolling. "What make you ask me that?" He pulled up to a red light and looked both ways.

"I don't know. I guess it seems like you and Kammron love this borough so much neither of you will ever leave it. But if you haven't noticed Harlem is getting worse. The crime rate is up by ten percent in this borough alone. The school systems are failing. They are finding lead in the majority of the pipes. The jobs are fleeing to other areas of New York, and stores are closing every single day. This is a dying community, not a flourishing one. For the record, us remaining here will do more harm than good, especially if you factor in us raising, Yazzy."

Bonkers shook his head and pulled past the green light. He imagined the looks and attitudes of the little girls in Harlem. Most of them acted way older than their years. They had bad mouths and were sexually active by the age of ten. The majority dropped out of school before the eighth grade. He wanted different for his daughter, he wanted her to have a chance. He wanted to make sure she was able to become anything she

2

desired to be in life. As much as he loved the hood, he didn't love it for Yazzy.

"Yo', that's definitely something we gotta talk about. I mean, I think I'ma get my chips right so I can move y'all up out of Harlem even if I stay. I gotta make sure my family is righteous, and well taken care of."

Yasmin held her silence, she felt angry. She crossed her arms and refused to look at him. Instead, she looked out the window as they rolled into the Taco King's parking lot. Bonkers peeped her change in demeanor. He pulled into the parking space, threw his truck in park and cut the engine.

"What's good, Shorty?"

She curled her lip and looked off. "Ain't nothing wrong wit' me."

"Yasmin, come on, ma. What's the matter? Did I say something that offended you?" He asked really wanting to know what was bothering her.

"Well, I just hate when you separate our family and get to talking that nonsense. I mean why would you move me and Yazzy out of Harlem, but you stay? That doesn't make any sense to me. I thought you said you were going to give our family a try."

Bonkers sat back in his seat and exhaled loudly. He looked over at her, and she avoided his eye contact.

He squeezed her thigh. "Shorty, a real man doesn't get to decide if he's going to man up and be a part of a family that he helped to create. It's his duty to be there for his family, and I am no different. I ain't thinking about separating us. I just wanna move y'all as soon as possible. I still got bricks and unfinished bidness in the hood. Once I fulfill my tasks, I'll be able to leave too, and I ain't never planning on coming back. But always and forever Harlem will be my first love. I got my first piece of pussy here. A li'l' thick ass girl too. All chocolate and what not," he teased, knowing he was referring to her. "I just gotta—"

Tishhhhhhhh! The passenger side window busted out. Yasmin was grabbed by the neck, and a gun was placed to her temple. "Break yo' muthafuckin' self nigga!"

Bonkers' window was the next to shatter. Then an AK47 was pushed through the window and into his neck. "Get the fuck out the truck bitch nigga, right now! Hurry the fuck up break yo' self!"

Bonkers felt the handle of his Tech 9 under his driver's seat. It took all of the willpower he had inside him not to grab it and get to spraying. He figured even if he was able go hit up the gunmen that had him hemmed up the other one would have a free pass to kill Yasmin, and he couldn't have that.

"Yo', a'ight, Kid. Y'all can have this mafucka. Just let me and my lady go." He placed his hand on the handle of the door. "Be smooth, Yasmin. You alright, baby?"

Yasmin felt the gunmen press the gun harder into her neck. A tear dropped from her eye. She swallowed and nodded. "Okay daddy, I'm cool, I'm cool."

The gunmen reached into the truck and pulled it open. He pulled Yasmin out and threw her to the ground. Then he kicked her as hard as he could into her back and stepped on her to get into the truck. Yasmin curled into a ball in excruciating pain. Next Bonkers' door was yanked open, and he was flung to the ground. The gunmen patted his pockets and robbed him of the fifteen thousand in cash he carried on him for sport. Then yanked the gold ropes from his neck, and kicked him in the ribs, before jumping into his truck, and peeling out of the parking spot. Bonkers wished they'd not been wearing masks. He wished he had some way of identifying them. He had never been more pissed in all of his life.

Yasmin made it to her feet, her back was killing her. "*And you wanna stay in Harlem!* Really—what the hell for? They coulda killed us!" she screamed.

Bonkers stood up and dusted off his pants. He eyed the brake lights of his Porsche truck, sucked his teeth and nodded his head. "A'ight niggas, it's good. This what niggas on? Yeah, a'ight." He could feel his heart turning cold as ice.

T.J. Edwards

Chapter 4

Kathy stumbled into the wall and caught her balance. She laughed to herself. "Damn." She made her way to the door and stood on her tippy toes to see out of the peephole. She saw Kammron standing there holding two big bags of groceries with a mug on his face. She took the three locks off her door and stood to the side of it.

Kammron stepped inside and looked around. As usual, her place was a mess. There was a stench coming from it that caused his stomach to turn. "Yo', open up a window in this ma'fucka a something, word up. I'm 'bout to spill my guts all over ya carpet."

Kathy rolled her eyes and staggered to the nearest window, opened it and sat against the ledge. She struggled to open her eyes all the way. She was higher than gas prices during the fourth of July.

"What brings you here, Kammron?" She scratched her inner forearm.

Kammron began throwing all of the old food that was inside of the refrigerator into the garbage can, before loading it with the new groceries he'd bought. "I'm yo' son. I ain't gotta have no reason for coming over here to see you other than I wanted to see you. It's as simple as that. Don't question me, woman."

She waved him off. "Well, I don't want you forcing me to eat. I ain't hungry, and don't know when I'ma be hungry neither." She turned her nose up at him and sat on the couch.

Kammron continued to stock the refrigerator. As soon as he was done he threw the grocery bags in the garbage and strolled into the living room. He grabbed her by the arm and sniffed. She smelled horrible.

"Yo', you finna get ya ass into the shower, Ma, word up. Yousa a Queen, you ain't supposed to be smelling like that." He pulled her toward the bathroom with her fighting against him.

"Let me go, Kammron! Get off me, I don't need no damn shower. You gon' ruin my high." She slapped him in the back of the head as hard as she could.

He took the blow in stride. "You getting ya ass in the water, I don't care what you saying. Your smell is ridiculous."

"Den leave my muthafuckin' house, you ain't gotta smell me. *Ain't nobody asking you to be here!*" she screamed.

She plopped to the floor and began throwing a tantrum. Her gown flew up and exposed her bony body. Kammron saw her ribs and grew weary. She looked as if she was fading away.

"Get up, mama, damn! I ain't trying to go through this with you today. You finna get yo ass in that water." He picked her up and carried her to the bathroom.

Her bedroom door swung inward, and a heavy-set dark-skinned man with bloodshot eyes stood in the doorway with his belly out. "Li'l nigga what the fuck is you doing with my woman? If you don't drop her, I'm finna drop you," he threatened, with a hammer in his hand.

Kammron mugged him and eyed the hammer in his hand. "Bruh, first of all, this ain't your woman this is my mother. And what the fuck is you doing in her bedroom with a hammer?" he snapped.

The fat man scratched his belly. "I'm standing here with no shirt, and my boxers on. What the fuck you think I'm doing? I'm helping her nail pictures to the wall genius." He laughed shortly. "Now, let my bitch go." He tightened his grip on the hammer and stepped toward Kammron with it.

Kammron jumped back with Kathy in his arms. He dropped her on the bathroom floor. "Get yo' ass up and get in the tub. I ain't gon' say that shit no more," he spat closing the door behind him.

"Kammron, I ain't washing my stink off me. This is my house, and you don't run shit in here. Now I'm your mother damnit! You gon' respect me. Chuck, please don't go there with my son. That boy crazy." She slowly got into the dry tub and kneeled down in it expecting the worst.

"Fuck this li'l' nigga. He gon' mind his bidness and we gon' mind ours. Bitch you mines, that's just that," Chuck growled prepared to do whatever he had too to put Kammron in his place.

Kammron eyed the fat man with his fists balled. "Yo', you think it's sweet to keep calling by moms a, bitch?" He eyed the hammer in the fat man's hand his heart was beating like a baller's trunk on a Friday night.

Chuck pointed the hammer at him. "Boy, you need to mind your bidness and stay in a child's place. You can't tell me what to call my bitch. This is her house, and you need to leave so we can finish doing what the fuck we were doing before you brought yo monkey ass here. It's as simple as that." He stepped toward Kammron getting pissed off. "That's what's wrong with you li'l' niggas these days, always in everybody else's bidness. Well, you gon' stay the fuck out of mine."

Kathy pulled open the bathroom door and stepped back into the hallway. "Chuck please lease this boy alone. He's crazy, please just listen to me. You don't know what you're getting yourself into," she warned.

"Kathy, don't play wit' me, bitch. Dis here is manly bidness. Now gon' get yo ass back in that bathroom. Gon' now, get!" He pointed with the hammer.

Kathy backed into the bathroom shaking her head. She closed the door. "Please don't do nothing crazy, Kammron. Please baby! He don't know no better. I'm begging you, Son, please. Y'all making my chest hurt."

Kammron was already thinking about the silenced Glock .40 in his waistband. He was imagining blowing Chuck's face right off his head and beating the remains with the nail extractors. A sly smile spread across his face. "Yeah, that sound like a plan."

Chuck mugged him. "Fuck you smiling at?"

Kammron upped the Glock from the small of his back and aimed it at Chuck. "Bitch nigga give me that mafuckin' hammer right now before I blow yo head off."

Chuck stumbled backward caught off guard. "Aw shit, say li'l' dawg—you ain't gotta go and do all of that. I wasn't finna do nothing with this hammer. I just wanted you to leave my lady house." He looked around crazily for an escape route. He felt as if he was in a frenzy.

Kammron cocked the hammer to his Glock and curled his upper lip. "Pussy nigga it's too late for that. Give me that hammer, right now!" he ordered.

Kathy stepped out of the bathroom and backed down the hallway away from them. "Kammron, baby, please. Please give him a pass for me. Please don't do nothing crazy. I know how your temper gets the better of you." She held her hand at shoulder level. "Calm down for me, baby, please."

Kammron aimed the gun at Chuck's forehead. "Yo', I'm giving you three seconds to hand me that hammer. If that ma'fucka ain't in my hand by then, I'm smoking you. Oh, and I ain't counting either."

Chuck felt the sweat come on his forehead. His heart was pounding like never before. He handed the hammer to

Kammron. "Huh, man, I swear I wasn't finna do nothing with it."

"Man give me this shit!" He yanked the hammer out of his hand and tucked his Glock into the small of his back. As soon as his gun was replaced, he turned the hammer around in his hand until the extractors were showing and swung it with all of his might.

Chuck felt the metal crash into his jaw and was met by the worst pain he'd ever felt in his entire life. The metal broke the skin and slammed into his bone-shattering it. The pain shot up to his eyeballs and watered them.

Then the excruciating pain resonated all over his body until he was screaming at the top of his lungs. "Awwww!"

Kammron yanked the hammer back and removed a massive chunk of Chuck's jaw along with it. The meat stuck to the extractors and dripped blood all over the carpet. "Nigga, don't you ever call my mother out of her name. That's my Queen, right there. You ain't got no right!" He swung the hammer again and planted it inside of Chuck's forehead. The hammer got stuck again, and Chuck had to wiggle it out of his face.

Kathy's eyes rolled into the back other head before she fainted in a heap in the hallway. Chuck tried to run as soon as the hammer was extracted. He made his way toward the front door, but Kammron was on his ass. He swung the hammer and smashed it into the back of his head. Blood splattered all over the wall and stained the pictures. Chuck fell to his knees, questioning why.

Kammron was in a murderous zone. He walked to the side of him. "My mother yo' bitch, nigga, huh? That's what she is?" He swung the weapon and beat the back of his head in with it, over and over again. "That's my, mama, that's my baby. She ain't nobody's bitch. *Do-you-hear-me-nigga?*"

Over and over he swung it until Chuck was left a mess in the middle of the floor.

Chuck felt like he was in the worst nightmare ever as the hammer beat down on him again and again. His high had completely left him. His body leaped from the floor as Kammron beat him senseless until the life dissipated from his body. His bowels loosened on him. Kathy woke up out of her slumber. She sat up and looked ahead and saw all the blood on the floor.

"Oh, my God, Kammron you didn't baby! Baby, you didn't." She got up and rushed into the living room.

Kammron was standing over Chuck with his heart pounding in his chest. He mugged the man's body and grunted, "That's what the fuck you get." He stepped on his chest, headed to the kitchen to grab an Apple juice out of the refrigerator.

Kathy kneeled beside Chuck, her eyes wide open. His face was mangled as if a hungry Lion had gotten a hold of him. The entire living room was flooded with his blood. It looked like a bucket of it had spilled over. "Why Kammron—why would you do this?"

Kammron downed the juice and tossed the empty container into the trash. "That nigga ain't have no right calling you out your name. He walking around this ma'fucka in his boxers and shit like he running shit. This ain't that, ma. You are my, Queen. I ride for you. How the fuck is he doing all of this anyway when ain't no food in the house, and I'm paying all the bills?"

Kathy looked at her hands that were saturated in blood. She felt a strong pulling in her chest, she shook her head. 'You're just like your fucking father, Kammron. He passed that gene on to you. That murder gene, and that bipolar shit. You ain't get it from me, that's all him."

Kammron waved her off. "You gotta say all that because I handled this nigga for you, really Goddess?" He walked over, picked Chuck up, threw him on his shoulder, and carried him into the bathroom. He dropped him into the tub and thought about how he was going to dismember him.

Kathy followed him. "This ain't right, Kammron. You can't take lives with no regard. He was a good man," she cried.

Kammron pointed down the hall. "Get yo ass out of here, ma. I don't wanna hear that shit about no other nigga. He gone, now deal wit' it, that's just that."

"Kammron, baby you can't keep—" A sharp pain shot up her left arm and made her heart feel like it was being stepped on by a sumo wrestler. Her breath became short, her vision went hazy. She fell to her knees, struggling to breathe.

"Mama, what's going on?" Kammron hollered, rushing to her side.

Kathy fell face first, she took a deep breath, as her vision faded to black, then she was lifeless.

T.J. Edwards

Chapter 5

Lightning flashed across the sky, as the rain fell from the clouds with a vengeance. The wind blew harshly causing the water to be used as a weapon. The constant pitter-patter of the rain hitting the ground was evident all around the cemetery. Kammron stood over Kathy's grave with an open bottle of Hennessey. He downed half of it and wiped his mouth even though his face was covered in rainwater.

Bonkers stood beside him with a heavy heart. The North Korean flowing through his veins caused his eyes to droop. He staggered slightly on his feet, as the lightning flashed across the sky for the fiftieth time, followed by a thunderous roar.

He placed his arm around Kammron's shoulder. "Yo', you got my sincere condolences, Kid. I can't even imagine what you're feeling, right now, but just know I am with you, and I am willing to do whatever it takes to get you into a better state of mind. We're in this shit together. Word to Jehovah man." He sniffed and wiped his nose as the rain beat on his back.

Kammron felt lower than dirt. "Yo', my, moms was all I had, Kid. Now that she's gone a nigga finna be lost in the sauce. My, word, shoulda pulled her off that shit a long time ago. That was my fuck up." He looked into Kathy's grave and saw her white coffin. The rain poured down and popped off it. The dirt around it had turned into mud. He could smell the earth all around.

"You ain't alone though, Kid. You already know we in this shit together. Kathy was my world, Dunn. She was my heart, too. I'm devastated right along with you." He faced and hugged him.

Kammron broke their embrace. "What, nigga you got a whole ass family now! A bitch that's finna be your wife one day. A daughter. What do I have? Not a soul in this world. You don't know the first thing about what I'm going through, Kid, let's just keep that shit real." He lowered his head and sighed.

He turned the bottle of liquor up, and swallowed a nice amount of it, before pouring some into Kathy's grave. He tilted his head backward, and the rain popped off his handsome face, and ran down his neck, drenching him. A bolt of lightning struck a tree about a hundred yards away from them, causing both men to nearly jump out of their skins. Bonkers upped his two Glocks on some paranoid shit. After being high-jacked at gunpoint while Yasmin was with him he'd been on constant edge.

Kammron fell to his knees in the mud. "Damn, mama, what the fuck was I thinking? I shoulda threw you in rehab, instead, I gave you the money to cop that poison, now you're gone. This ain't your fault, its mine. I should be in that grave, not you. You are a Goddess, a Queen. I shoulda protected you better. Now all I'm stuck with is that crazy old man. Fuck I'ma do wit' him?" He broke down, as the rain picked up its velocity.

Bonkers stood beside him for a second before kneeling down. He could feel the mud squish into the knees of his Burberry pants. He would have to get rid of them, and they'd cost him over five hundred dollars. He placed his arm around Kammron's shoulders and rested his forehead against his.

"Yo, word to Jehovah man, you got me. I'll never put nobody before you, Kid. You're my family, we been family. You're not alone, Dunn. Please know that. Ain't nobody gon' stop me from holding you down. That's on my soul, Kid."

Kammron couldn't stop tears from falling from his eyes. He stood up and threw the bottle of Hennessey across the graveyard.

He reminisced on how his mother looked when he last physically laid eyes on her. "My moms' was so skinny, man. That dope and shit ate her up. How the fuck did I let this happen? What kind of son am I? I ain't shit man!" He pulled out his gun and placed it to his temple, cocking the hammer.

"Oh shit!" Bonkers jumped up and took hold of Kammron's wrist, disarming him with one move. "Fuck is you thinking, bruh? You gotta be strong."

Kammron fell to his knees beside the coffin, feeling the soft mud stain his Gucci pants. He placed his hand on the coffin. "She was only thirty-four years old man. *Thirty-four years old*, and she's already in the grave. What type of shit is that, Dunn?"

Bonkers stood up and shook his head. He hated seeing his right-hand man going through so much pain, emotionally struggling with the thought of letting his mother go. "Yo', you go ahead and grieve, Kid, then let's get the fuck out of here. Jimmy got a move that's gon' bring us some serious dough. I need you by my side the whole way."

Kammron pulled Kathy up again and hugged her body tighter. "I love you, mama. I swear I love the shit out of you. I'll never forget your many sacrifices. I'll be there real soon to protect you." He stood back. "Yo', everybody finna feel the wrath of my mother's death, Kid. You hear me, Bonkers. I'm on some no mercy shit. Anybody can get it. So, you need to know that when you're conducting bidness with me that is how I'm getting down, period! You got that shit?" he snapped.

Bonkers replied, "Yo', it is what is. You already know, I'm rolling with you however you wanna do things. But for, right now, how about a change of pace? Let's go and see what's good with, Jimmy. He gon' put us up on some much-needed cash, then we can probably take a vacation a something. What you think about that?" He asked as lightning flashed across the sky. He still held Kammron's gun in his left hand.

"At this point, I'm willin' to try anything." He looked into his mother's grave and shook his head. "Let's get the fuck out of here. And give me my gun back, I'm good now."

****

Jimmy sat at the head of the long table that was covered in a white table cloth. On top of the table was an assortment of foods: Fried chicken, Glazed ham, pinto beans, white rice, cornbread, a seven up pound cake, and a bunch of condiments. Jimmy's maid, a thick, redbone came up from behind him and tied a Gucci bib around his neck. She kissed him on the cheek and walked off with her forty-inch ass cheeks jiggling under her short skirt.

Kammron couldn't take his eyes off her ass. He felt his manhood stir. "Yo', shorty thick as a muthafucka. Ain't no way I could have her working under me. I'd stay in that pussy, straight back shots, too."

She looked over her shoulder at him, smiled and ran her tongue across her lips, before heading into the kitchen to start her cleaning regime. The scent of her perfume remained in the dining room. It was a scent that left each man feeling some type of way.

Jimmy placed two thighs of fried chicken on his plate and dumped baked macaroni and cheese next to it. "Once you get your cheese all the way up, Kammron you'll have bitches like that eating out of the palms of your hands, all day long."

Kammron placed two breasts on his plate and added white rice, and pinto beans next came the cornbread. "Well, I hope we're a lot closer then we think. I'm ready to have bitches like that kissing my ass even when I got gas." He looked over at Jimmy from the corners of his eyes.

Jimmy had his hair braided into four long French braids. They fell across his chest. He was rocking a Gucci robe, over Gucci pajamas, with matching Gucci slippers. "Kammron, you making it seem like y'all ain't eating a something. I thought I was handling my bidness for both of y'all?" Jimmy said, smacking.

"Yo', you are big bruh. Ever since me and Kammron linked up with you, I ain't seen no less than fifty gees for taking home every week. So, you definitely doing ya thing, Kid," Bonkers assured, drowning his chicken in Tabasco sauce.

"Speak for yourself, Kid. I ain't staying in some big mansion. and I ain't got some foreign broad placing bibs around my neck and shit. So, nall I ain't eating the way I'm supposed to be. This is New York, Kid. If mafuckas ain't seeing at least a few million you ain't doing shit. Nowadays a few million ain't shit but lawyer money. So, yeah, I'm hoping that we're about to be straight sooner than later." He picked up a drumstick and ripped the meat from the bone with his teeth.

Jimmy felt somewhat offended. Kammron had a habit of always striking a nerve with him. He tried his best to calm down. "You know I been putting in a lot of work to be sitting in this position. I been making connections all over the fuckin' world. It ain't easy to be sitting in this position. I wish it was."

"I mean you might be making a bunch of phone calls to handle your end of things, but when it comes to being in the field that's all me and bruh. We cause that bloodshed and pave the way for you to live how you living. All I'm saying is I wanna reap more benefits than you are. Seem to me like you're sitting back like a fat mack." He ripped more of the meat from the bone, and chewed it with his eyes closed, smacking loudly, savoring its juices. "That foreign bitch can cook."

Bonkers was seconds away from jumping into the conversation so that both men would focus on other things. He knew they barely liked one another, and it was imperative he kept the peace. He needed both of them. He didn't trust anybody more than Kammron. He knew he would kill for him in a heartbeat, and vice versa. He needed Jimmy as well. Jimmy was sure to help them get into a better stature in New York. He had a lot of connections, that would soon pay off.

Bonkers was sure of that. "Yo', we just gots to be patient, Kammron and trust Jimmy. He got us, bruh. Kid finna put Harlem back on the map."

"I ain't got no problem with that." Kammron downed the Wildwood Soda Pop and burped loudly. "I just wanna know how long this shit finna take? I ain't got no patience. You already know how it is in New York, it's here today, and gone tomorrow."

Jimmy wiped his mouth and tried his best not to wild out. He had to take the high road because he knew he needed Kammron and Bonkers. They were his trusted shooters even though Kammron was a bit of a head case. "Yo', respect, Kammron. I know you a true Harlem nigga and you just wanna get your bread up. That's understandable, and real soon you'll be able too. Just stay the course. In three weeks, I'ma fly you niggas out to Jamaica wit' me, and we gon' holler at Stunna. He the one that had them Brooklyn niggas eating before the indictments came down. He's looking for a new borough to take over New York, and I'm looking for that borough to be Harlem. If Kid fuck wit' us the long way, we'll be eating like fat bitches when they get their food stamps."

Kammron nodded. "Now that's what I wanna hear. All you gotta do is tell me what to do and it's done."

Bonkers sighed in relief, happy the conversation had taken a turn for the better. "Yeah, what he said."

"Well we got some work to clean up where them Brooklyn niggas left messes, but y'all leave the logistics to me. Just have them burners ready, and it's gon' be good that's my word. We about to fall into some serious dough, so much that Kammron gon' praise the Kid."

Kammron grunted, "Yeah, we gon see about that."

Jimmy laughed. "A'ight, long as I can confirm we can move into that slot then everything will be good. It's a process, but I'll be sure to make it happen in that time frame. In the meantime, I need you two to lay low. Y'all gotta remain under the radar as much as possible."

Bonkers didn't see that being a problem for him. If need be, he would stay inside the house with Yasmin on some lovey-dovey stuff. He was sure she would love that. "I can do that, what about you, Kammron?"

Kammron burped again and scooted away from the table. "Yo', long as it's some major chips involved, I'll be smooth. I don't like them Brooklyn niggas no way."

Bonkers laughed. "Me neither, nigga. They hoes cool, but the niggas think they the shit. It's time Harlem become the epic center of New York again."

Jimmy smiled and held up a bottle of Moët. "Let's do this shit for Harlem then. Resurrection to the borough of heaven, here, here." They toasted and finished their meals with money on their minds.

T.J. Edwards

Chapter 6

Yasmin turned on the vacuum cleaner. He sat up in bed and grabbed his Tech from under it, still half asleep. He aimed at the doorway and groaned as his head began to spin. Woke less than ten seconds and already the drug began to cry out for him. He rubbed his face and sat the Tech on the bed after coming to his senses. He sat there for a moment and slid out of it, found his stash spot in the third drawer of his dresser and took it out. He poured a small amount of the North Korean on to the dresser top and tooted it hard. Then he poured a bit more and repeated the process. He pulled on his nose and swallowed, poured just a tad bit more of the drug and leaned his face down to toot it up.

Yazzy's presence in the doorway threw him off. He jumped up and stood in front of the drug. "Hey, baby girl? What are you doing woke already?" he said in his most cheerful voice.

Yazzy held her teddy to her chest. "Daddy, what were you just doing?" she asked with her head turned to the side.

Bonkers felt like crap, he was hoping she hadn't caught him in the act when in actuality she had. He didn't know what to say. He'd already vowed he would never lie to his daughter, and he was going to stand by that. "Baby, get over here and give me a hug." He ordered with a big smile on his face.

She dropped her teddy bear, ran full speed, and jumped into his arms. Her arms tightened around his neck before she kissed his cheek. "I love you, daddy. I love you so much," she repeated over and over again.

Bonkers held her, and low key cleared up his tooting area. He brushed the residue of the North Korean from his dresser top and hugged his daughter tighter.

53

"I love you so much too, Boo-Boo. Let's go in here and see what your mama doing." He carried her down the hallway.

When they got to the end of it, they saw Yasmin dancing in the middle of the carpet with the vacuum cleaner in her hand. Her tight cleaning shorts were all up in her booty. The dark brown cheeks jiggled as she danced in her own world. She popped her back and looked over her shoulder at them, she jumped from the shock of their presence.

She pulled her earbuds out of her ear and turned off the vacuum cleaner. "Damn, y'all scared the crap out of me. Bonkers you know better than to be running up on me like that," she chastised him.

Bonkers snickered. "That's my bad, shorty. We watched you cut a rug, and I got stuck. I see yo li'l' ass getting thicker, too. That's what's up."

She smacked her lips. "I been eating, that's all that is." She turned back on the vacuum cleaner and continued with her tasks.

Bonkers kissed Yazzy's cheek again and set her down on the floor. "Baby, go play for a minute, and let me holler at mama, okay."

Yazzy groaned, "Awww-uh. Can I come back after you get finished then?"

He nodded. "Sure, baby, that's cool. Now gone, I'll come get you when we're finished." He kissed her cheek again and hugged her.

Yazzy slowly mopped down the hallway with her head bowed. She took one sad look over her shoulder at him, and stuck her bottom lip out, before turning away and following his orders.

Bonkers waited until she closed her door before he tapped Yasmin on the shoulder. She jumped once again, and nearly fell over the glass table. "Damn, what the fuck is wrong wit' you?"

"Nall, shorty what's wrong with you? You seem like you got something going on, what's really good?" Bonkers questioned taking a hold of the vacuum cleaners handle.

Yasmin shrugged her shoulders and yanked it away from him. "I'm good, Bonkers, damn." She went back to vacuuming the carpet.

The vacuum cleaner left streaks in the carpet each place that she ran it as it cleansed the carpet. She grabbed the bottle of carpet freshener off the glass table and sprinkled it in each area while she vacuumed. Yasmin was a stickler for keeping their place nice and clean. She had a habit of waking up first thing in the morning and cleaning the house from top to bottom. It was one of the many things Bonkers loved about her.

Bonkers looked her over from a few feet away. He tried to think about anything that he had done over the past few days that coulda had her feeling some type of way negatively toward him. He couldn't think of anything no matter how hard he racked his brain. In his mind, he had been on his P's and Q's. He knew Yasmin did this thing where she would keep her feelings, and thoughts bottled up inside instead of coming to him right away when there was a problem. Then when things would build up so deep within her that she could no longer take it, she would finally blow and reveal a week worth of frustrations blowing his mind. This had become a habit of hers. She would go on and on about something that happened so long ago that it would infuriate him. It was one of the things he disliked about her. He walked slowly in the direction of her with his arms spread apart.

Before he could make it all the way there, she shut off the vacuum cleaner and mugged him. "Now what Bonkers?"

He stepped into her face, took a hold of her small waist, brushed the loose curl from her forehead, and looked into her eyes. "Baby, talk to me, I'm here to listen."

She looked into his face and pursed her juicy lips. "I ain't got nothing to say, it is what it is."

Bonkers took a deep breath, he was trying his best to remain calm, and not wild out because of the attitude she was giving him. He knew he had to be patient, and kind with her even though both attributes were the furthest things from his interior make up. As much as he hated to admit it, he'd developed some strong feelings for Yasmin. He loved waking up in a household where it was him, her, and his daughter. It made him feel like they had their little family all put together. It was a feeling of completion that he was looking to get used too, especially after growing up in a broken and abusive household.

Most of the families in Harlem grew up in a single parent, usually a struggling mother, household. He wanted different for Yazzy. He wanted to give her a fighting chance, and he knew it started with his relationship with Yasmin. He held her and looked into her pretty face again.

"Baby, yo, you can tell me what's good. I swear, I ain't gon' wild out on you. I'ma hear you out, and respect where you coming from, word up. All you gotta do is tell me what's good."

Yasmin looked him over closely to see if she could tell if he was trying to set her up just to get information. She knew his temper was lethal. She truly wondered if she could trust him at his word.

She decided that she couldn't. "Bonkers ain't nothing wrong with me," she lied, after deciding she would deal with her emotions in her own way. She'd been that way her entire life.

Bonkers wasn't buying her lie, he rubbed her shoulders. "Come on now, baby. How are you and I going to move forward with our family and be better than our parents if we can't even be honest with each other? Now I know something is bothering my woman. I wanna know what's good? I should be your safe haven. We should be able to come to each other about anything fearlessly. Now come on, tell me, Boo." He kissed her cheek, softly.

Yasmin popped back on her legs and crossed her arms in front of her chest. She sighed, "Alright, but you can't get mad either, after all, you promised?" She looked him over for any signs of frustration and appeared to find none.

Bonkers was thirsty to know what was good. He nodded his head and crossed his heart with his index finger. "Alright, now damn, tell me what's really good?"

She took a step back and took a deep breath. She was trying to build the courage deep within to confront him. She really didn't like confrontations. She exhaled slowly. "Okay, Bonkers, when were you going to tell me you were planning a trip to Jamaica without me or your daughter?"

Bonkers was shocked. "How the hell do you know about that? I ain't even had the chance to come to you about it yet.

Yasmin once again had to find the courage deep within. "Honestly?"

He nodded. "Yeah, honestly. How do you know about that?"

"I went through your phone when you were in the shower. You should already know I'm crazy about you. I just wanted to see what was good with my man. That's when I ran across the texts from Kammron talking about y'all trip to Jamaica, and how y'all finna be fuckin' a bunch of bad Jamaican bitches, while you're bussing plenty of moves." She punched her hand. "The bussing moves part doesn't bother me. I know how you get down, and I'm cool with that. But the fuckin' a bunch of bitches part got me vexed, word up."

Bonkers felt like blowing a gasket. He balled his hands into fists and mugged her with mounting anger. "Shorty, what I tell you about goin' through my phone?"

"Oh, no don't try and turn this thing around on me. First of all, you said you wasn't going to get mad, so you can't. Secondly, we both agreed to keep things one hunnit with each other in the interest of our family. You fucking with a bunch of Jamaican women ain't keeping it one hunnit while we sit back here in Harlem and worry sick about you. It's not fair," she snapped.

"Yo', calm yo ass down. I never said I was finna slay none of them hoes so don't put words into my mouth, or actions on me that I ain't did." He stepped out of the front room and into the kitchen. "I don't like when you do that shit either." He paced back and forth and didn't know what to do. He felt like Yasmin had overstepped her bounds by going through his phone.

She stepped into the kitchen. "You ain't have to say you was gon' do nothing, Kammron already said it for you. If he fucking a bunch of thotties then you will be, too. Y'all are birds of a feather. Two peas in a pod, the whole Harlem know that."

Bonkers flared his nostrils. "Yo', I ain't on none of that shit that Kammron on, we got a whole ass family. This deal in Jamaica could make us some very rich men. That's all I'm focused on. This money could help me move our family out of Harlem for good." Bunkers didn't like being micromanaged by anybody, not even his woman.

Yasmin could sense he was deeply troubled and trying to maintain his temper. She didn't like upsetting him. She felt Bonkers had the potential to be a good man. She just needed to get him away from Kammron. She stepped up to him and touched his shoulder. "I'm sorry for going through your phone. I'm just so used to be around trifling men, from my father on down to my brothers, and the few I have come into contact with. Yazzy needs us to make it, and so do we. Please don't be mad at me. Are you?"

Bonkers closed his eyes and exhaled through his nostrils. He forced himself to calm down. "Look, I know you been through a lot, so I won't hold this offense against you. But you gotta trust me. I know that's easier said than done, but you have to try. I actually give a fuck about you, and Yazzy, and want the best for all of us. I wanna invest in you and expand our business. I wanna move our family out of Harlem for good. I wanna get to the point where I can take my ass back to school. I don't wanna be stuck in the hood forever." He backed up into the refrigerator, and butt dialed Kammron's cell phone.

"But baby you already know how, Kammron is. He'll smash anything that look like something. He's a bad influence on you, always have been. I mean, I ain't trying to say nothing bad about yo mans, but I feel he is going to be the detriment of our family."

Bonkers lowered his head in anger. "Can't no nigga make me do nothing that I don't want, too. I'm getting grown, and it seems like the more grown I get the further apart I am growing away from bruh. I got a family now. Y'all are the first thoughts on my brain every morning. Not him, or the streets. That street shit is still in me, but sooner or later a boy has to become a man. I don't know how much longer me and Kamm gon' be tied at the hip." He felt defeated when recognizing that truth.

Yasmin squealed, "Oh, baby, I can't believe it! I never thought you would choose nobody over, Kammron. That's always been my biggest fear when it came to our family's longevity. So, to hear this is just—uh!" she screamed and hugged his neck. "I love you, daddy. I love you so much!" she squealed.

Deep down she knew Bonkers was the man for her. No other man had ever made her feel like he did just by being in her presence.

"I love you too, Boo, and always know nobody will ever come between us, and our family. Y'all are my life, and nothing and no one means more to me than you two do. I'm riding for y'all because that's my job as a man. You ain't got shit to worry about, I promise you."

"But what if you had to choose between us and Kammron, then what baby? I know you gon' choose your mans, but where would that leave, me and Yazzy?" Yasmin asked, fearing the worst.

Bonkers shook his head. "Never that, I will always choose you two." He hated even thinking like that.

Kammron was his heart and he knew if it came down to it he would have a hard time choosing anybody over him, but at that moment he knew Yasmin's heart had to be eased. She appeared vulnerable, it was his job to protect her both externally, and internally.

"I got you, Boo, for the rest of my life. It's us, I promise!"

Yasmin had tears in her eyes, she felt so emotional. All she wanted was for their little family to work. Kammron was the only person standing in their way. She couldn't wait until Bonkers dropped him like a bad habit.

"Long as I know we come first it eases my worry. Always choose us, daddy. Please, and with that being said I trust our family to you for always." She closed her eyes and held his neck.

Bonkers rubbed her back. ''Don't nobody exist outside of y'all, period, this is us.'' He felt like a sucka for saying those words to her but knew they were needed. In his heart, he knew he would ride for Kammron until his last breath.

****

Five blocks away, Kammron stood with his phone to his ear and a mug on his face. He couldn't believe the words coming out of Bonkers' mouth. He knew he had to get rid of both Yasmin, and Yazzy real soon. They were imminent threats to his and Bonkers' friendship, and he refused to lose his right-hand mans to a broad. The thought alone caused him to become irate.

Chapter 7
Kingston Jamaica

It was a bright and humid day. The sun shined from the clear from blue sky with a vengeance. Its rays heated the atmosphere and brought forth a heat that was uncomfortable for all three men. Jimmy cruised through the Ferrari lot with a Burberry book bag, containing two hundred thousand dollars. He stepped up to a cherry red Ferrari and walked around it with a big smile on his face.

"Hell, yeah, I'm finna have these Jamaican hoes pussy wetter than a bitch in heat after they see me in this ma'fucka," he jacked, adjusting the shoulder strap of the book bag. He pressed on the driver's side door, and it flipped upward like a Lamborghini. He gasped, and sat behind the steering wheel, looking over the dashboard that reminded him of a spaceship from the movies. "Aw hell yeah." He inhaled the air hard and relished in the scent of the new car smell.

Bonkers stuck his head inside of the car. "Say, Kid, I thought we was down here strictly on bidness. Why you copping ships and shit?" He wanted to know.

The sun rays beamed off the back of his neck. It felt like it was trying to fry him. The air was so thick he was freaking himself and thinking that at any moment he wouldn't be able to breathe.

"Yo, when you conducting bidness wit' heavy hitters you gotta look the part. I can't pull up to a meeting of sorts in anything less than a muthafuckin' Ferrari, Kid. It's just how the game goes, word to Janine. I gotta have this joint fa the stay down here," Jimmy said, already making his mind up.

Kammron circled around a black on black Lamborghini. He flipped open the doors and fell in love with the all-white leather interior. "Harlem in the muthafuckin' building. Yo',

Jimmy we staying down here for a week, right?" He asked sticking his head out of the whip. He sat back down and rubbed all over the leather seats. "Yo', I wish I could push this bitch down one fortieth and Lennox. Them chicken heads a fuck around and break they neck to see a nigga." He imagined the girls back home in Harlem doing just that and cheesed.

Jimmy stepped over and peeked his head inside if the Ferrari Kammron had become obsessed with. "Yeah, Dunn, we booked for a full week. What you feeling this li'l' ho, right here?"

Kammron stood up. "Boy-boy, and you know this. I gotta have this ma'fucka, right here. I can see myself fucking one of them thick ass dark-skinned Jamaican hoes in the front seat, while her friend suck all on the back of my neck." Kammron closed his eyes and nodded his head. "Yo, den I'ma have to take her ass down, too. We finna set this boy on fire. Hello Jamaica!"

Jimmy busted out laughing. "At least I know you gon' have a good time while we down here. Now, all we gotta do is get my li'l' brother to loosen up, and we'll be good." He rolled his eyes and pointed with his head at Bonkers who waved him off. "Anyway, y'all gon' need to decide on which whip y'all want me to cop. I can only get two total cause these joints are crazy expensive. They want they cash up front, too. These Rastas down here don't play about their dough. So, what's good?"

Bonkers shrugged his shoulders. "It don't matter to me. If this the one Killa want, then we can roll this boy. I'll chill in the passenger's seat and let him get his shine on. It's all love." He shook up with Kammron and gave him half of hug.

Kammron broke the embrace and beat his chest. "We finna set this bitch on fire. Ya Mon!" he attempted his best Jamaican accent.

Jimmy laughed, and carelessly rested his hand on top of the roof of the car and pulled back. The roof was so hot it felt like a fiery skillet to him. "Fuck!" He shook his hand out and placed it under his arm to cool it off. "Yo', I'm finna go and cop these bitches. Y'all chill, and don't get into any trouble." He headed in the direction of the dealership's rental office.

Bonkers pulled on his nose. "Yo', it's time to get right, Kid. But it's so hot down here I'm scared to go handle my bidness." He could feel his body craving North Korean. He tried his best to shake it off. "I don't like being too high, and too hot at the same time. That shit makes me miserable."

Kammron began to relay the conversation that he'd overheard Yasmin and Kammron having a week ago. He still couldn't believe his right-hand man was planning on deserting him for a bitch. He felt like his heart had been broken. He was hoping they spent an ample amount of time down in Jamaica so they could restore their old childhood relationship.

"Yo', we finna wild out down here, Kid. It's so many hoes down here that we ain't finna know what to do. And they be knowing how to fuck. It's like they mothers teach 'em that shit at a young age or something. Son, I can't wait!" He got giddy imagining the possibilities.

Bonkers smiled. "Yeah, me neither," he lied.

Smashing a broad was the furthest thing from his mind. All he could think about was the fact that he was missing Yazzy, and Yasmin already. He wanted to get back to New York, and to his girls. At the first opportunity, he had plans of ducking off with his phone so he could Facetime with both of them. He wanted to make sure his family was okay. Harlem was getting crazier and crazier by the day. They were his first priorities. So, even though he was currently in Jamaica, his heart was back in New York with his family.

"Yo', I'm wit' you, Kamm, let's have some fun."

****

Kammron switched gears and stepped on the gas pedal. the Lamborghini jerked forward and sped down the highway. He flew pass cars with a whipping sound. He nodded his head to the music blaring out of his speakers and laughed at the top of his lungs.

"Yo', I'm pushing this joint to the limit, Kid! It's out world, ours, Bonkers. Live fast, and die young, Dunn, word to Kathy." He swallowed the lump in his throat and shook his head.

Bonkers sat back with his head on the headrest, as Kammron zipped passed car after car at blazing speed. He had the top to the Ferrari lowered. The wind brushed across their faces and only added to the excitement for Kammron. He laughed and turned the bottle of Moët up. Then looked over at Bonkers nodding, before swerving to the next lane, blowing his horn at a busted pick-up truck that was following the rules of the road. Then he swerved around it and stormed down the highway, holding the bottle of Moët in the air.

Bonkers shook his head. "Yo', Kammron, I know you trying to enjoy ya self, and get ya stunt on and all of that good shit. But Kid, maybe you should slow down before you get us killed. You're already punching over a hundred miles, B."

Kammron stepped on the gas pedal even harder. The Ferrari roared like an angry Panther. It lurched forward and began flying pass the other cars on the highway that were following the rules, leaving them with a cloud of smoke from the pipes behind the car.

"Nah, Son fuck that. Yo', you know I got this knob, Kid. I been whipping cars ever since I was nine years old. That used to be our hustle in Harlem. You remember that shit?" He drank a large portion of the Moët and swallowed hard.

Back when Bonkers and Kammron were kids, and fresh off the stoop, their first move had been to steal cars and turn them into the chop shop Jimmy worked for back in the day. Jimmy would give them a list of cars he needed them to get, and the boys would spend all day long hunting for those particular ones. After they brought them back to the shop Jimmy would give them two hundred dollars a-piece for each one. When they were nine, ten, and eleven, ending the day with close to six hundred dollars seemed like a lot of money.

"Yeah, Son, I know you got that whip game proper, and all that shit. But we're in Jamaica, Dunn. We don't know how these Rastas down here run their jail, but I can only imagine they shit ain't right. Nah, mean?" Bonkers looked over his shoulder for any signs of the long arm of the law.

Kammron snickered. "Yo', the last thing a nigga worried about is winding up in some Jamaican jail. Them mafuckas a have to catch me first. And as long as I'm pushing a Ferrari, that shit ain't happening, word up." He flew in front of a Cadillac, and almost caused the driver to veer off the road.

The driver behind the wheel blared his horn at him again and again and waved his fist out of the window.

Kammron held up his middle finger and kept going. The sunlight caused his forehead to shine bright. He looked in his rearview mirror and laughed. "Yo', that nigga Jimmy was robbing us blind back in the day."

"How so?" Bonkers asked, looking over his shoulder to make sure the driver they'd nearly ran off the road wasn't about to pull out a gun and get to bussing.

"Yo', because now that I think about it." He turned the Ferrari hard and caused it to scurry against the pavement. The pipes roared, then he was flying doing a hundred and ten miles an hour. "Yo', Kid was only paying us two hundred dollars for each whip, when all along they were giving him twenty-five hundred for each whip we brought to him. That was robbery, Son no matter how you look at it." He looked up ahead and saw he was going to need to maneuver around four cars if he was going to hit his exit on time.

Bonkers thought about that for a moment. He remembered how they felt back then when they found out Jimmy had been getting over on them all along. He remembered having to calm Kammron down because he was thinking about taking him out of the game, but Bonkers was strongly against it. "Yeah, I remember how all that went down back then, but it's all good now. We're grown, and we ain't taking no shorts or losses, B. Ain't no sense dwelling on the past, it ain't gon' help our future one iota. Nah, mean?"

Kammron squeezed between two cars, stepped on the gas and made a hard left that got the Ferrari to fishtailing. Smoke billowed from the wheels, as he slammed on the brakes, just as soon as he did so, he was stepping on the gas again. He jolted, and sped on to the exit ramp, then reduced his speed just in time for the red light at the top of the hill. His heart was beating fast, as he looked over at Bonkers and smiled at him.

Bonkers mugged him and broke eye contact. "Yo', you be wilding, Kid, straight up."

"If Jimmy was playing us back then when it came down to the cars and a few other things. How do we know he ain't doing it again? I mean think about it, Kid living in a fucking palace compared to what we living in? And he's making all the transactions. We don't really know what he seeing, all we know is what we're getting. That shit from when we were shorties still left a pretty bad taste in my mouth." A car behind them proceeded to blowing its horn. Kammron eased pass the green light, into traffic. He was headed toward the beach.

Bonkers didn't want to delve into the past. They were in Jamaica. That was a long way from Harlem. Jimmy was at the wheel, and he was forced to trust all of their best interests were at the forefront of his brain. "Yo', I don't wanna get into all of that, Kammron. All we can do is hope, bruh, keeping shit on the up and up. If we find out he ain't then we gotta be done fucking wit' him, it's as simple as that."

Kammron nodded in agreement. "Yeah, bruh I feel that. Sooner or later we ain't gon have to worry about whether Jimmy keeping it one hunnit or not. We'll be doing our own thing. It's always been just you and me Bonkers. Always, and we ain't never needed nobody else. Now we got all these people in our lives that don't need to be there. My word, I wish we could go back to being Kids again. Shit was so much simpler back then."

Bonkers was silent for a moment. Then he looked over at Kammron. For some reason, he felt Kammron was no longer talking about Jimmy, but he was low key speaking in terms of Yasmin, and Yazzy. Bonkers knew he could not bite the bait. He was a long way from home. The last thing he wanted to do was be beefing with his right-hand man.

"Yeah, I wish we could go back to being kids, too, but we can't. So, we gotta make the best of everything the way it is now. Yo', you touch bases with Shana yet?" He was trying his best to change the subject a little bit.

Kammron shook his head. "Nall, Kid, shorty still missing in action. I'm sho' she'll turn up soon. She probably just worried that a ma'fucka gon' do something to her because of her knowledge of what happened to, Shelly. She think a nigga out of his mind, B, hoes crazy." Kammron laughed and took another long swallow from the Moët.

Bonkers felt his high lowering. He covered his face with both hands and closed his eyes. "She ain't the only one. I think you're out of your mind most of the time, too. But I still love yo crazy ass. Always have, always will."

Kammron pulled the Ferrari into an empty parking space at the beach. Even though it was only nine in the morning it was already packed with people ready to get their swim on. There were thick Jamaican women walking around in small G string bikinis. Their asses shook with each step they took. Their breasts nearly spilled out of their tops. Their skin looked freshly oiled. Tattoos decorated some of their bodies, while others were pure in appearance. Kids ran back and forth, then into the water, splashing it. While men walked around dark-skinned and shirtless, their abs on full display along with their bulging biceps, and long dreadlocks.

"Yo', if that's the case, if that love is real, Kid, then we gotta get back to the basics. We gotta get back to putting each other first and allow the rest to fall under that. You're all I got, Bonkers. I ain't finna let nobody take my brother away from me." He extended his hand. "It's us right, dawg? First and foremost."

Once again Bonkers truly felt Kammron was taking a shot at his family and even though he thought about checking that shit, he knew Jamaica was not the place to do it. He shook Kammron's hand and gave him half of hug. "It's us Kid, first and foremost."

Chapter 8

Jimmy hopped on the four-wheeler and revved the engine. He looked to his right and saw Kammron just hopping on top of his, and to his left, Bonkers was doing the same. Behind them was six of Stunna's security guards. The men were heavily armed and had patted down Jimmy, Kammron, and Bonkers before they were allowed to enter the trail of where they would be meeting Stunna in the woods. All three men were able to rock their Kevlar vests though. Jimmy felt good about that because even though he knew this was a business meeting he never could wrap his head around trusting crazy Jamaicans.

He rolled the handle of the four-wheeler backward and increased his speed making sure he kept up with their guide, a long, dread-headed Jamaican who looked like he carried whole engines around all day long. Jimmy had money on his mind. He felt if he could fulfill the vacant spot that had been left by the Brooklyn crew because if their many indictments, he could take his borough of Harlem to the next level. It was millions to be gained. That was money he was not willing to pass up under no circumstances. He hopped over a tree branch and revved his engine.

The woods as expected were dominated by tall trees. Since the sun was beaming like crazy the atmosphere was swampy and moist. The heat was dry and made each man with the exception of the locals feel miserable. All three men sweated profusely along their foreheads, and down the backs of their shirts. The bulletproof vests only added to the heat. Kammron navigated with a mug on his face. There were so many bugs flying around that more than once they'd crashed into his face, and lips. He was itchy and felt paranoid because he was traveling into a place he had never gone before. He prayed Jimmy knew what he was getting them into. Jimmy's decision making held their lives in the palm of its hands.

Bonkers drove with his eyes lowered into slits. He couldn't get Yasmin off his mind. He missed her so much even though it made him feel some type of way to admit. He missed Yazzy just as much. He wanted to be back home with his family. He knew the only way he could assure they were straight was if he was there looking over them at all times. He was hoping the meeting with Stunna went smoothly, and they could get the hell out of Kingston, Jamaica, and back to the United States where his people were.

Jimmy continued to cruise. The guide came upon a big cave and stopped his four-wheeler. He hopped off it, walked over to Jimmy and placed his hand on his shoulder. He was dark-skinned, skinny, with long gray dreadlocks, and red eyes that looked like they belonged to a bull. He smelled of sandalwood and Ganja.

"Say Mon, it's about tree blocks in dis hur cave. Us follow me. If ya loose course dares men in dare dats trained to fill us wit' holes. Dats a mistake you don't wanna make homeboy. Tell ya comrades, and let's be out." He jogged back to his four-wheeler.

Jimmy looked back at both Kammron, and Bonkers. "Y'all heard that shit right?"

Both men nodded in unison. A swarm of gnats circled around them. Birds flew overhead just as two squirrels ran in front of them and disappeared into the woods rustling along the way. Kammron smacked a bug on his neck, and wiped it away, two more flew into his ear canal buzzing loudly. It irritated him so bad that he wanted to scream bloody murder. Bonkers was busy swatting at a bunch of them as well. They had crashed into his cheek more than once. He was over the whole woods thing already.

"A'ight then, let's be out," Jimmy ordered turning around and guiding them into the cave with Stunna's security guards behind them.

There was just a hint of light when they first entered, then it got dark, and felt murky inside. There was a strong stench of feces, and piss. It smelled like a cold project stairwell. Jimmy flipped on his lights and kept pace with the brake lights that were in front of him. Their four wheelers whirred through the cave. Splashing up the dirty water, and emitting clouds of exhaust into the air. Big rats ran alongside the path their beady red eyes glowed when the lights from the ATVs cast upon them. The further they got into the cave, the stuffier it felt until Jimmy, Kammron, and Bonkers felt like they were losing oxygen at an alarming rate.

"Yo', how much longer we gotta travel in this ma'fucka, B? I feel like I can't breathe!" Kammron hollered.

Jimmy ignored him. He didn't know that answer and he was not trying to lose sight of the guide in front of him. He'd already seen them Jamaican assassins ducked off in the crevices of the cave. They looked almost scary with their green and black war paint. They held machetes in their hands or assault rifles. Jimmy couldn't lie to himself, he felt nervous. If things were to go haywire there was no way he would be able to get them out safely, and alive. He was placing all of his trust inside of a Jamaican that he was quite unfamiliar with. That was one of the golden rules of the game broken. You were never supposed to place yourself at the mercy of another man, by doing so you fully render them your fate. He shook his head and remained determined. It was all or nothing. There was no such thing as turning around.

Finally, after ten minutes of rolling through the swampy, horrible smelling cave, they pulled up to a barrier that was guarded by eight of Stunna's heavily armed security. One, in particular, stepped forward and aimed his AK-47 at them. The guide got off his four-wheeler and bowed his head.

He then turned around and pointed at all three men. "They are Stunna's guests. I've been given my orders to bring them directly to this cave."

The guard looked past his shoulder. He mugged the Harlem natives and grabbed his walkie talkie. After reporting what was taking place at the entrance of Stunna's bunker, he was given the order to allow the men to pass. He waved them to follow him and clapped his hands together at his workers. They rushed and rolled the stone wall aside. Seconds later Kammron, Bonkers, and Jimmy rolled through it, along with Stunna's appointed men.

****

Jimmy brushed a beetle off his arm and scratched the spot it had previously crawled on. He didn't understand the Jamaicans and how they could put up with the bugs all day long. He wanted to get the hell out of there. He had been waiting inside of the stuffy room for nearly two hours alone before the stone door pulled open, and three guards stomped inside shirtless with machetes in their hands. This caused Jimmy to go on high alert. He stood up, ready to panic, reached on his waist for a gun but found it empty.

"Fuck, this was a set up all along," he snapped ready to fight to the death.

The guards surrounded him, they looked maniacal and angry. Like they were ready to kill something. Jimmy looked around for any weapon of sorts, the only thing his eyes laid on was a bunch of rats. They screeched and scurried underfoot.

Jimmy threw up his guards. "Yo, you muthafuckas ain't finna do shit to me without a fight. This Harlem, son, word to Janine."

The guards closed in with their machetes raised. Stunna stepped through the door and held up his hand. "Back off!" The five feet three-inch man hollered. He was dark skinned, with dreadlocks that dragged against the ground. His eyes were bloodshot red, he looked extremely muscular.

The guards backed away from Jimmy and took their posts with their backs against the wall. Their machetes were at their sides. They were hungry for the American blood, yearned for the kill. But Stunna called the shots, and until he gave them the order they would lie in wait, fiening.

Stunna walked up to Jimmy and extended his hand. "So, you're the Harlem representative?"

Jimmy shook his hand. "The one and only. I'm the man that's about to help you reconquer New York. I can stand on that."

Stunna laughed. "Me don't need any help in conquering any ting my boy. Conquering is in my bloodline. My father and his father was conquers of dis here island you stand on, right now."

Jimmy looked around, he saw bats by the hundreds hanging upside down at the very top of the cave's room. "Yo', dis don't look like no damn island to me. It looks like a fuckin' cave. Yo', no disrespect but no matter what understanding we come to today, I ain't never meeting you back in this ma'fucka. This too creepy."

Stunna smirked and walked around Jimmy. He motioned with his hand for him to have a seat, which Jimmy did. "Let's get one ting straight, right now, Harlem. If I decide to do bidness with you you'll do what I say, and how I tell you to do it. There are quite a few boroughs trying to find their entrance into me, and my powers that be. Me don't need some cocky, arrogant, idiot telling me when and where he's going to conduct business with me. That's not how the game works, especially when I am the game." He sat across from Jimmy at the round table that had been set up for their meeting.

There was a shimmer from the light outside the door, it illuminated Stunna's neck. For the first time, Jimmy saw that the man was wearing over three million dollars in priceless jewels. His neck was draping with gold that had diamonds encrusted all over it. Jimmy grew envious right away and felt he needed to slow his role.

"Yo', that's my bad, Stunna, you're absolutely right. If this is the place you want to meet, I have no problem with that. It's your world, baby."

Stunna stood up, waved him off and laughed. "N'all boy, me have dis cave as much as you do. It's itchy, bugs are everywhere, and everywhere that the bugs are not there are the rats, and other creatures that have stumbled inside to torment us." He paced, and Jimmy could hear the sound of his jewels as they clinked. "But it's wartime, it tis currently a struggle for, Jamaica. The island is in high demand. But no matter what takes place, Jamaica belongs to me. Let me make that very clear, Jimmy. I'm not hiding out, I am simply regrouping." He turned and came back to have a seat at the table. "Why should I choose you instead of some other hustler from dee states? What makes you so special for, Stunna?"

Jimmy cleared his throat. "For one, I get money, Son. I know New York like the back of my hands. I know all of the power players and the low-level niggas. I can take the merch that you was giving them Brooklyn niggas, and double what they were bringing back, while at the same time avoiding that indictment list. I got brains, Kid."

Stunna shrugged his shoulders. "Who gives a fuck. Me don't care about ya brains, or who you know. It's not that hard to figure out who the players of New York are. What else you got?"

Jimmy frowned, he lowered his head and rubbed his chin. "I can give you a million dollars up front, and we can go hard from there. I'm telling you, you are talking to a supreme hustler. I'm the type of nigga that—"

Stunna cut him off by slamming his hand on the table. "Me don't give a fuck about none of dat shit, Harlem. Money will come and go, dats not why I approve dis meeting. Me need more dan dat," he snapped.

Jimmy felt himself becoming irritated, his face flushed red. He balled his fists and tried to calm down. He looked over into the angry face of Stunna. "Since I ain't hitting the right chord with you man. Why don't you just tell me what you're looking for? Why did you approve this meeting?"

"For blood!" He slammed his hand onto the table again. "I got wind that you niggas in Harlem are lethal. Relentless bombaclat that don't hesitate to take a life when it comes to your cash. That mirrors Kingston, that mirrors, Stunna! That's what I want on my team. Those muthafuckas from Brooklyn were pussies. Now they are all rolling over on each other like it's something normal. Their actions make me fearful to deal with New York again. Den me hear dis ting about you boys in Harlem, and it makes me smile. Me tink it's cool to give ya Borough a chance, as long as you can stand at the head, Jimmy." He stood up. "I'm familiar with Ruiz, and his work back in Cuba, and New York. Ruiz is a good man like myself. He's a money maker, he's lethal and he takes no pity! That's your bloodline, that's dee kind of man I'm looking for."

Jimmy nodded and sucked his teeth. "Then you found him, right here. Me and my boys are about that life as long as it's plenty of paper involved. We'll show you Harlem is unlike any other borough. All you gotta do is say what you need done, and we'll show you."

Stunna shook his head and laughed. "It's war time here in Jamaica, Jimmy. I have one enemy, his name is, Flocka. In Kingston, we look to make a statement before the guard can be passed, or a war is considered finished. I personally want Flocka's head. You get me his head and clean up the mess in Brooklyn before it spills over to Kingston, and we have a deal. I'll help you become bigger than your father Ruiz ever was. You have my word on that, and in Jamaica, a man's word is all he has."

Jimmy nodded his head and rubbed the hairs of his chin. "You give me the blueprints of this Flocka person. His whereabouts, and some other things, and you sit back and watch how Harlem goes into action." Jimmy was ready to prove his worth to Stunna, and entire Jamaica if he had too.

He needed the man on his team. It would be the only way he could place Harlem back on the top of the totem pole the way it needed to be.

Stunna stood and shook his hand. "You'll have everything you need, and when you are finished here in Jamaica a party will be thrown in your favor." Stunna smiled. "I am sure you are going to love that."

Jimmy ran his tongue across his teeth. "Business before pleasure, let's get this show in the road."

Chapter 9

"Yo', I still don't understand why we gotta put all this paint on our face and shit. What's wrong with doing shit the Harlem way? Ski masks ain't never bit us in the ass before," Kammron grumbled, as Jimmy painted his face half green, and half black so they could blend it with the locals that would be at the big parade that night.

Jimmy made sure he copied the picture from his phone that Stunna gave him. He wanted to make sure everything was in place. He understood the Jamaicans in Kingston played for keeps. One false move and not only would he, and his boys he slain there in Jamaica, but he was sure it would spill over back to the United States of America. There were too many crazy Jamaicans in Kingston that it was ridiculous.

"Yo', Kamm, we can't do shit the Harlem way, right now because we ain't in Harlem. We're in Jamaica which means we gotta do shit their way or else we're going to stick out like a sore thumb. Now, Stunna, said this parade we're going to tonight has been thrown specifically for us to do what we have to do with, Flocka, and his henchmen. After we get him separated from his loyal ones I'ma waste him, and we gon' get the fuck up out of Kingston. When we get back home, we got a li'l work to do with those Brooklyn cats before our connection is made back here to the island.

"Though it's a process, in the end, it spells millions of dollars for all of us. Now, I know y'all tired of hustling packs, and working with the bare minimums, all the while looking over your shoulders. Well, connecting with Stunna is the first step to putting an end to all of that." He finished the job on Kammron's face, and stood back, washing his hands in the sink.

Kammron rushed to the mirror and looked himself over. He didn't like the reflection looking back at him. "Yo', I hear everything you're saying Jimmy, but I swear I hate this shit being on my face. Only females use makeup. I can't see how these Jamaican cats run around rocking this shit all day long." He felt so irritable. He was hoping the paint didn't break him out.

Bonkers stood behind him and cheesed. "Calm yo' as down, Killa, you ain't the only one rocking this shit. Look at ya boy, right here," he ordered, placing his arm across Kammron's shoulder.

Kammron looked him over from the reflection in the mirror. Saw that his paint reflected his. That made him feel somewhat better, that was until he remembered the conversation he'd overheard between Bonkers and Yasmin, then he felt cold toward Bonkers. He tensed up and moved from under Bonkers' arm.

"Yo', whatever man, let's just get this shit over and done with so I can wash my face." He bumped Bonkers a tad as he made his way out of the big bathroom, and back into the hotel room.

Bonkers felt some type of way. He mugged the back of Kammron's head and stood there for a moment looking him over with curiosity. He couldn't fathom how rocking the war paint could make him feel so weird. After all, they were set to do a job. He shook his head and turned to Jimmy.

Jimmy shrugged his shoulders. "Yo', don't sweat it, Kid. You already know how Kammron gets down, he's a weird one." He placed his heavy hand on his shoulder. "The sooner we can handle this bidness the sooner we can get back to New York. Come on."

"Yo', I'll be with you in a minute. Let me use this bathroom real quick, I got the bubble guts," Bonkers lied.

Jimmy nodded and left out of the room. "We leave in twenty minutes."

As soon as Jimmy stepped out of the bathroom, Bonkers closed the door. He turned on the sink, both temperatures as high as they could go, then the shower, before pulling out his cell and calling Yasmin.

Yasmin was sitting on the couch reading Life Of Sin on her cell phone when Bonkers' call came through. She sat upright and answered it, "Hello, Baby, is that you?"

Bonkers sighed, "Yeah, ma, it's me. How are you and my baby girl doing?" he asked feeling his heart melt.

Yasmin's eyes were misty. She couldn't believe how bad she was missing him. It had only been a week, but for her, it felt like an eternity. "We're doing fine, baby. Missing you like crazy, and I'm trying my best to stay sane. I can't help worrying about you every single second, of every day. I need you, Bonkers. I just want you to know that." She sniffled and wiped her nose.

Bonkers sat on the closed toilet seat and lowered his head. "Damn, baby, I swear I miss you just as much. I'm trying to finish things up here, so I can get back to you, and Yazzy. We're about a day or so out, I was just calling so I could hear your voice. I'm starting to need that from time to time." He felt so sappy admitting that, but it was the truth.

Ever since Yasmin had come back into his life, he felt like he had new meaning. Like he had a reason to live outside of the ghetto. That made him feel some type of way.

Yasmin sucked on her bottom lip, she didn't know what to say. She knew this was Bonkers way of being vulnerable, and she didn't want to say the wrong thing. "Baby, I just want you to know your family is here for you. We love you, and we are waiting for you. Do whatever you have too, then get home. Please, because we need you. Just know that, okay, baby."

Bonkers nodded and held his forehead. "Yeah, ma, that's what's up. Kiss our baby for me, I'll be there in a minute. That's my word."

Yasmin felt he was about to hang up the phone. She didn't know what he was up too, or if she would ever see him again. That thought alone was causing her stress levels to rise. "Bonkers, I love you!" She waited as her heart did somersaults. She was praying she could hear him say the words back to her. Those words would mean everything.

Bonkers squeezed his eyelids together. He shook his head from side to side. He knew he loved her already. That he was crazy about her, but the thought of actually saying those words would make him feel so soft. He took a deep breath and no longer cared. He would throw caution to the wind.

Kammron beat in the door and threw it open. He caught sight of Bonkers sitting on the toilet with the phone to his ear. Frowned, and already assumed who he was talking too. That vexed him. "Yo', Kid, it's time we roll out. Tell shorty ass you'll fuck with her later," he spat.

Bonkers jumped up. "Baby, I'll get at you in a minute. We gotta go handle some bidness." He disconnected the call.

Yasmin's eyes closed as she heard the phone line die. A lone tear escaped her eyelids. She held the phone to her chest and began praying to God for the safe return of Bonkers.

****

Jimmy leaned all the way back in the passenger seat of the Rolls Royce Phantom. He adjusted his fatigue jacket, and looked over at Stunna, as the parade took place half of block away. He could hear the loud pounding of the drums, and the music blaring in the streets. Even from that distance, he could make out a bunch of dancers as they shook their asses to the beat uninhibited, wearing next to nothing.

"Ya do dis job da right way, Mon, and me promise you'll be filthy rich," Stunna assured him as he smoked on a White Owl cigar stuffed with the best ganja on the island of Jamaica.

Jimmy felt the handles of the blades inside his coat pocket. "Aw, you ain't gotta worry about nothing. I'ma handle my bidness, so we can keep moving forward, and my boys gon' handle theirs. But I do have a question for you." Jimmy sat up and looked over the parade. It appeared to be getting more and more packed.

Stunna took a big pull of the blunt and inhaled deeply. "What's dat now, boy. You kin ask me any ting."

"Why us? You got all kinds of Jamaican killas all around you every second of every day. Why not use one of your own to take care of, Flocka?"

Stunna shook his head. "Jamaican blood cannot spill Jamaican blood. Dats not how the guard is passed. The killing must come from an outsider, and the island cannot find out about it. If day were to find out it'll spell trouble for me for generations to come. Dis is why I invest in Harlem. It's crazy, but it's Rasta politics. Besides Flocka is my older brother. Once he is out of dee way, then I will be King."

Jimmy nodded his head. "Aw, now I see. The only way you can become King is if Flocka is slain?"

"Yes, he holds the keys to the throne of our bloodline. My father has three weeks to live, then all of his fortunes and connections will be passed on to Flocka as is our customs. Flocka will, in turn, help me to strengthen my standing in dee underworld, but fuck that, Mon, me kant wait to be dee, King. Me ready, right now. Blood or no blood. As soon as me steps upon the throne I bring along me son Solomon, dee Golden Prince. He was me father's favorite. Dares good tings ahead for me bloodline, you watch and see. Me tell ya no lies." He took another pull from the White Owl and blew smoke from his nostrils. The smoke filled the interior of the car and caused it to become cloudy.

"Flocka, next in line, huh?" Jimmy asked, looking out at the parade.

Stunna laughed. "Dat don't sound like it's gonna happen now does it?"

Jimmy pulled the serrated blade from his inside fatigue pocket with blazing speed, tightened his grip around the handle, before slamming the knife into Stunna's thyroid. He pulled it out, and slammed it back into him, twisting it. There was a loud sound of Stunna's throat popping as his vocal cord was punctured, then his esophagus. Again, and again Jimmy jugged the knife inside of the man until he slumped over with his head inside of his lap.

"Then ain't no reason for me working for you, Kid. I only fuck wit bosses! Yo', days are over." He jugged him in the back of the neck, then pulled his head back and reached inside of his mouth, taking a hold of his tongue, before he cut it out, as were per the wishes of Flocka.

****

Bonkers pulled open the limousine's door, and took a step back, lowering his head. Solomon came from the house with his neck flooded draped in ten gold chains that were flooded with ice. Solomon was Stunna's firstborn son. His dreadlocks fell down his back. He held a fat, freshly rolled White Owl in his right hand, stuffed with yellow Ganja. He looked Bonkers up and down, and turned his nose up at him, before sliding into the back seat of the stretch Escalade.

Bonkers waited for him to get inside before he entered himself. He sat across from Solomon with his heart pounding in his chest. He could taste the salt in his mouth. His palms were sweaty, as he looked at the ground in front of Stunna's son.

"Hey, say Mon, turn the damn air conditioner up. Me like the temperature at a certain degree!" he hollered toward the driver of the Limo. He waited a few seconds. Then reached and began to bang on the partition. "Say, Mon, did ya hear me?"

Kammron rolled down the partition. "Yeah, muthafucka, I hear you. I'm the last one that's gone hear you, too."

Bonkers hopped from his seat and slammed the blade into Solomon's neck from the side, wrapped his arm around his forehead and fell backward with him, jugging away. His blood popped into the air over and over, wetting Bonkers' war paint.

Kammron busted out laughing and stormed away from the curb. He turned up the reggae on the radio, and nodded his head, eyeing Bonkers in action through his rearview mirror. "Yo', Kid, I'll cut his tongue out. You can't be doing every fuckin' thing." He turned up the air conditioner as high as it could go. "Say, Solomon, you catching enough air back there?" He laughed again.

Bonkers jugged him ten more times and sat back on his haunches. He wished he didn't have to stab him so much, but Solomon kept moaning and groaning fighting for his dear life. He looked down at him and wiped the blood from his mouth. "Yo', he through, Dunn. Hit up Jimmy and tell him it's done. All you gotta do is get his tongue, and we can get the fuck off the island."

Kammron was already texting away on the burner phone. "Sounds real good to me. These Jamaicans ain't so hard, B. These mafuckas bleed just like we do."

****

Later that night

Flocka stepped up to Jimmy and placed both of his hands on his shoulders. "What you done did here is priceless, and it will not go unnoticed. Me take the throne in three weeks. In three weeks, I will make sure you understand how much I appreciate you. How does that sound?" Flocka asked looking into his eyes.

Jimmy picked up the duffle bag full of cash he'd already received as a gift from the Jamaican. Inside was five hundred thousand dollars in cash, in all kinds of bills. Jimmy raised the bag shoulder level. "Well, we'll take this as a token of your appreciation for now. But I'll look forward to your word. Let's get Harlem back where it used to be." He gave him half of hug, before jumping on the private jet alongside Bonkers, and Kammron headed for New York.

Chapter 10

It was two and a half weeks later. Bonkers awoke to the feeling of Yasmin climbing over his body. She straddled him, and looked into his handsome face, rubbing his naked chest with her small hands. "Wake up daddy and bless me with those sexy brown eyes," she flirted.

Bonkers smiled and yawned. "Yo', what's good, Goddess, what time is it?" He looked toward the window in the bedroom and saw the sun had not had the chance to fully rise.

"It's five in the morning. Yazzy, still sleep, and I want some of my man. Actually, I'm fiending for you. You been pulling one all-nighter after the next ever since you got back from Jamaica. I'm starting to feel some type of way." She leaned down and sucked on his neck.

Bonkers felt his piece stretching already. It didn't help matters that it was first thing in the morning, and he was already experiencing a morning wood. His dick was so hard it hurt. "Baby, what you trying to do? You know, Yazzy, a be in here in a minute."

She kissed down his body, felt between his thighs, and gripped his dick. She squeezed it, before pumping it up and down. Then she was kissing and licking all over the head, sucking it into her mouth hungrily.

Bonkers breathing became labored. He rested his hand on her hair, and ran his fingers through her lace front, gripping it just enough. "Damn, baby, you finna make me murder that shit."

Yasmin moaned with him inside of her mouth. She sucked up and down his pole, sliding her hand between her thighs, and teasing her clit, sending chills up and down her body. "Mmm."

Bonkers reached across her back and slapped her fat ass booty. He squeezed it, and trailed his fingers down into her crease, after pulling her short Fendi nightgown above her waist. Her chocolate ass cheeks were on full display. Once he located her pussy lips, he slipped a finger into her hot hole and felt like it tried to swallow the digit.

"Mmmm, daddy, that feels so good. It's been so long!" She spaced her knees apart and really went to town sucking him while she held him in her fist, pumping.

Bonkers humped up from the bed. He stretched his arm so he could dig in her pussy hole. Finally, the feeling between his legs became too much. He needed her, he had to feel that choc- olate pussy wrapped around his piece. He was fiending for it. He released her hair and pushed her off his dick. "Ma, get ya ass up here and ride this dick, or I'm finna fold ya ass up and really hit that thang. Come on."

Yasmin felt tingles emanate all over her. She imagined Bonkers fucking her senseless, and it made her pussy so wet that her essence began to seep out of her. "Eat this pussy first, Bonkers. Please daddy, please! I need to feel your tongue, right here." She spread her sex lips and pointed at her clitoris. "Daddy, can you please just—"

Bonkers flipped her over onto her stomach and forced her right thigh to her rib cage. Once there, he forced his face into her middle, and slurped her labia into his mouth loudly, as if it were oysters. Yasmin groaned and spread her thighs further.

She reached under her thighs and exposed her pink insides. ''Get it, daddy, get it, right now, please!''

Bonkers licked up and down her slit. He trailed circles around her clitoris. The nub felt wet and slippery. He sucked it into his mouth and ran his tongue back and forth across it, over and over.

Yasmin shivered. "Unnhh, Daddy-unnnhh. It feel so good, it feels so good, Daddy." She humped her pelvis into the mattress, and groaned deep within her throat, as Bonkers' tongue ran circles around her rosebud. He held her open and literally sucked on her crinkle, sliding his tongue back and forth inside of it.

Yasmin arched her back, and let out a guttural moan, before cumming hard. "Uhhhhh, daddy—Daddy, Dadddeee!"

Bonkers kept her clit trapped between his lips. His tongue skid back and forth across it. He could feel her jerking like crazy. This excited him all the more. He pulled her on to her knees, and sucked her from the back, while she played with herself. He licked all over her salty fingers. Even taking the time to suck on the digits one at a time.

"Fuck me, Bonkers. Please, fuck me, right now." She fell on to her back and opened her thighs wide. She ran her fingers up and down her sex lips, before sliding two inside of herself. Her nipples were spikes sticking through the Fendi gown.

Bonkers pushed her knees to her chest and got in front of her. He stroked his pipe and slid the head into her opening. Her heat engulfed him at once. Then he was long stroking her at full speed, fucking her Harlem style while the bed tapped at the wall. Her pretty toes were over his shoulders, thighs were against his chest, as he hammered away at her box.

Yasmin was beside herself. "Uh-uh-uh-uh, Dadddeee! Yes, yes-ooo, baby-Bonkers-uh-fuck—slow down, Daddy. You hitting this pussy too hard. You hitting it too hard, Daddeee!" She laid the side of her face on the sheet and licked the cloth. She didn't know why she did it. She was just feeling freaky. Bonkers had a way of bringing her inner whore out. She was a whore for him, and never minded being one for him either. "Uh! Shit!"

"Uh-uh-uh, this my pussy. Mine-fuck, Boo. Tell daddy—whose pussy-uh-uh-uh, dis is-argh!" He sped up the pace and went as deep as he could over and over.

"It's yours—yours daddy! Awwww-Daddy, Mmm, I'm cumming—I'm cumming again. aww, shiiittt!" She dug her nails into the sheets and scratched at them.

Bonkers fucked her so hard that it hurt his abs. Her pussy was good to him. It was hot, wet, snug, and the scent was driving him crazy. He could still taste her on his tongue. That fact only added to his arousal. When he felt her tugging on his manhood with her inner walls it became too much. His balls ascended into his lower abdomen, then he was cumming hard.

"Arrrggh, baby, here Daddy come." He bust back to back, lubricating her walls with his seed.

****

Kammron leaned his seat all the way back, as he made his way past one fortieth and Lennox at nine o'clock in the morning on a nice Fall day. Something told him to look to his left, and as soon as he did, he slammed on the brakes. The sight of a pregnant Shana entering into the bodega on the corner of 142nd was enough to cause him to go into action. He sped to the curb, then jumped out of the car, slamming the door, and taking the keys out of the ignition.

Shana looked over her shoulder as she heard the tired screech along the street behind her. When she locked eyes with Kammron through the windshield of his Porsche, she nearly shitted herself. She broke into the store, nearly knocking over an elderly woman. *"Help me! Help me! He finna kill me!"* she yelled.

The Arab cashier grabbed his gun from under the counter and looked toward the door. "Girl, why are you screaming. Whose supposed to be killing you?" The older man asked.

Shana ran up to the counter and pointed at the door. "Kammron, he coming, right now. He's crazy, please help me!"

Kammron brushed past the elderly lady that was picking up her spilled oranges. He rushed up the steps to the bodega and pushed in the door. The bell sounded, he scanned the store until he found Shana standing in front of the cash register shaking like a wet dog, on a cold Winter night. He slowly made his way toward her.

Shana felt like she was about to lose her mind. She could only imagine what Kammron was about to do. She held up her hands, with tears falling down her cheeks. "Calm down, Kammron. I can explain everything, all you gotta do is give me the chance."

Kammron closed the distance between them with light-ning speed. He grabbed her hair and yanked her head back-ward. "Shana where the fuck you been? You been missing in action for damn near two months."

She cried out in pain, it felt like he was ripping her hair out by the roots. "Ow, please, let me explain what's going on."

"Hey, you muthafucka, you let her go, or I'll put a cap in your ass! How does that sound?" The Arab cashier asked hold-ing his gun over the counter so Kammron could see it.

Kammron tightened his grip in Shana's hair. "Nigga, if you don't put that gun away, I'll have this mafucka burnt to the ground. This one, and that gas station of yours up the way. This is Harlem, Kid, I'm Killa, Kamm. This my shit, word to streets." Kammron felt his heart pounding in his chest. He was seconds away from upping his gun, and bussing until his clip was empty.

The Arab shook his head from side to side. "I can't do that, release this woman and let her go on her way. You get the fuck out of my store or else."

Kammron tightened his grip on her hair once again. Now he was heated. "Or else what?"

The Arab store owner pointed his gun at him and cocked the hammer. "Or else I'm going to empty this magazine to your black ass and tell the cops you tried to rob me and this woman, right here. For God sakes she's pregnant." He held his gun tighter. "Now let her go!"

Kammron mugged him for a long time. "Bitch ass Arab, this ain't got shit to do with you. This between me and my bitch. I'm telling you, you're making the wrong move."

"I'm giving you until the count of ten to leave my store, and I'll begin counting, right now. One, two, three—"

Kammron released Shana. "Bitch, this what you finna do?" You finna make me go through all of this shit just so I can holler at you?" He was beyond vexed. He didn't care how things wound up in the end, he was going to burn the Arab's store, and gas station to the ground. He no longer wanted it in Harlem.

Shana trembled, her knees knocked together. "Are you going to kill me, Kammron? Be honest with me."

Kammron shook his head. "My word to, Kathy, all I wanna do is holler at you, Goddess. You and I need to get an understanding for our child's sake."

"Five, six, seven—" The Arab continued to count.

Kammron opened the door mugging the man. "Come on, Shana, come the fuck wit' me real quick." He did his best to look as soft as possible, though on the inside he was seething. Every part of him wanted to slay the store owner for pointing the gun at him.

Shana was wondering if Kammron would kill her like he had her sister Shelly. She wondered if he'd also convinced her to follow him to some remote area before he took her life. That thought alone caused her to shake in fear. But on the flip side, she knew Kammron wouldn't go away. She needed to get an understanding with him. Needed to let him know she wanted to move on with her life without him. That every time she saw him, she only saw Shelly's face. She needed to get all of that off her chest.

Kammron backed to the top step of the porch and held the door open for her. "Come on, shorty. This shit can only get worse before it gets any better." He held his hand out to her.

"Don't go, honey. You can stay here for as long as you need too. I smell trouble with this one," The store owner warned.

"Come on, baby, fuck dude. Let's get an understanding, I promise I won't hurt you."

Shana lowered her head and sighed, "Okay, Kammron, just please keep your word.

****

Jimmy grabbed the bags of groceries from Janine's arms and jogged up the stairs to the stoop of her apartment out in Harlem. He made it to the top step, and juggled them in his arms, while she traveled up the stairs behind him. "Yo', moms, you got all types of gallons of milk, and orange juices in these bags. Please for me, put a li'l' pep in your steps," he joked.

Janine slammed her hand on her hip and smacked her juicy lips. "Boy, ain't nobody tell you to grab all those bags out of my hand. You're the one trying to be Superman, not me." She took the keys to the house out of her pocket and made her way up the stairs to the stoop. Janine was five-feet-two-inches tall. A hundred and forty pounds, with caramel skin, and brown eyes. Her hair was natural, shoulder length, and bumped at the ends. She had a taste for expensive fabrics because of her son Jimmy who insisted on spoiling her.

Jimmy's eyes got bucked as he saw the two red Bentley trucks storming down the street. Then they slammed in their brakes in front of his mother's crib, and Showbiz, one of the Brooklyn dope boys hopped out with a Tech in his hand.

"Say, Jimmy, we need to talk homeboy!" Showbiz hollered.

He ran up the stoop and placed his arm around Janine's neck. Behind him were his crew of savages. They hopped out of their trucks heavily armed and stood at the bottom of the stoop waiting on any signs of unrest from Jimmy. Showbiz had already given them the order to shoot if they felt he was in danger because Jimmy was a dangerous man.

Jimmy held up his hands. "Yo', that's cool, B. Just let my, moms go in the house, and I'll roll off with y'all, it's as simple as that."

Showbiz was light-skinned, with hair just as long as Jimmy. He kept it pulled back into a silky ponytail. His eyes were light brown, he stood tall and muscular. Like Jimmy, he had Cuban blood flowing through straight from the heart of Havana. He was the son of the infamous Vito Vega. Jimmy knew the Vega family was deadly, that if they had sent their oldest son to accost him, it spelled trouble.

Showbiz released Janine. "We don't hurt women unless we have too, Jimmy, you know that. Let's go." He rushed up the stoop and took hold of Jimmy.

Janine dropped down, with her hands on her face. "Don't hurt my son, please don't hurt my son!"

As Jimmy was being ushered into the back of the truck, he took one last look back at his mother. "Yo', it's good, Goddess. Just gon' in the crib. I'll catch you later, Love, word up."

Showbiz stuffed his head inside of the truck, and they peeled away from the curb, headed to a duck off in Red Hook.

T.J. Edwards

Chapter 11

Kammron paced back and forth in front of Shana. Every other second, he would look down at her with an angry mug on his face. He was trying his best to calm down. On top of that his high was wearing thin. He needed a pick me upper. He could feel himself crashing all over his body. His head felt like it was pounding. He stopped mid-pace and took a deep breath. Shana sat on the couch with her head lowered, and her knees spaced apart so her pregnant belly could rest right between her thighs. She was shaking as if she were cold, but the temperature of the house was perfect. Her shaking came from fear. She didn't know what Kammron was going to do next.

"Alright, Shana, you been sitting there for ten whole ass minutes without saying a word. Your silence is starting to piss me off in the worst way. I need to know where you disappeared, too? Who took you in? And what the fuck you told them about, Shelly's disappearance? Don't lie to me either because you know one way or the other I'ma find out. Now tell me what's good?" He slapped his hands together, loudly.

Shana jumped a bit and looked up at him. "Kammron, you are off your rocker. You're not right in the head, somethin' is seriously wrong with you."

Kammron smirked and ran his hand over the top of his waves, he felt uneasy. The one thing a mentally ill person hated to be told was that they were off their rocker, or out of their mind. For him, that was an instant trigger to go ape shit.

"When I found out about what had taken place with, Shelly, it spooked me. She was my sister, Kammron, and you killed her. That was mind-blowing. I couldn't be around you without feeling sick on the stomach. So, I left. What did you expect me to do?"

Kammron mugged her. "Bitch, I get all of that, and that is perfectly fine. I ain't got no papers on you, but one thing I wanna know is who took you in? Where did you go? And what did you tell them?"

"My father took me in, he stays on Staten Island. I ain't have to tell him nothing. He didn't tell my mother where I was because they don't jam like that, and I told him not, too. I got my own room there. I stayed to myself up in it, it was as simple as that."

Kammron looked her over carefully. "Then why all of the sudden you wind up back in Harlem? Why you ain't stay out on Staten Island with yo old man?"

Shana lowered her head. "He found out I was pregnant. He snapped, choked me out, and kicked me back out. Told me I was a whore like my mother. That I disgusted him, he threw me, and my few articles of clothing on his stoop and slammed the door, typical him." She shook her head and swallowed the lump of pity in her throat.

Kammron pursed his lips. "Man, shorty you tryna give a nigga that sob story, so I don't get all in that ass, right now. You already know I'm less than two seconds from fuckin' you up. How you gon' run off with my seed like that? That ain't cool in the least bit."

Shana's mouth felt drier than a desert. She tried to swallow her spit, but she was suffering from cotton mouth. She smacked her lips together. "I need some water, Kammron, my throat dry as hell." She stood up and made her way into the kitchen. She ran the sink and filled her glass halfway, before sipping from it.

Kammron came behind her and turned her around. "Tell me why I shouldn't get all in your ass, Shana?"

Shana looked him over from the rim of her glass. She drank the water slowly trying to choke up with a reason.

Kammron was so heartless. It was hard to penetrate his emotions, and she truly wondered if he actually had any.

Kammron smacked the glass from her mouth. It crashed into the wall and shattered. Then he grabbed her by the collar of her shirt, and slammed her into the refrigerator, knocking off four boxes of cereal, and three loaves of bread that were on top of it. They came falling on top of her head. "Bitch, I'ma ask you again. Why shouldn't I be getting all up in your ass, right now?"

Shana closed her eyes and tilted her face away from him. "Because you said if I came back here with you, you wasn't going to do this. But I knew I shouldn't have come back here. If you murdered me, it wouldn't be nobody's fault other than my own." She opened her eyes, and tears ran down her cheeks.

Kammron mugged her with anger. "So, you telling me the whole time you was out, you didn't tell anybody what happened to, Shelly?" He breathed into her face. He felt his sick coming on harder, he needed a fix.

"Kammron, if I told anybody what you did, you'd be in jail already. That shit ain't in me. I loved my sister don't get me wrong, she was my heart. But after she found out me and you were messing around behind her back she said some pretty rough things to me that cut deep to my soul. For instance, she told me after I had my child she was going to kill me. She swore that on our grandmother's grave. And you know what I believed her. That's why when she was alive, I was trying to save my money so I could get the heck away from here. Second to that, yo, I'm from Harlem. I'm thorough, I know how to keep my mouth closed as if I got lockjaw. I would never tell on you for what you did, I would kill you first." She trailed her eyes up to his and peered into them, fearless.

Kammron snickered. "Oh, is that right, you'd kill me, huh?"

Shana was tired of playing Prey. She no longer wanted to be the victim. If Kammron was going to kill her then that's just what it was going to have to be. But she would go with her head held high. She smacked his hands away from her. "You muthafuckin', right. Get off me, Kammron." She pushed him back.

Kammron stumbled into the sink and busted out laughing. He held his stomach and fell to one knee cracking up. Even if he tried to stop his self from laughing at that moment he couldn't. What was crazy was that he didn't even know what was so funny.

Shana took a step back and looked him over. She didn't understand what was going on. His laughing only infuriated her. She felt he was refusing to take her seriously. That was insulting to her self-esteem. She pulled open the knife drawer and pulled one of the big ones out of it. "Kammron, if you ever put your hands on me again I'ma show you better than I can tell you. That's on my mother. We gon' have to deal with each other for a long time because of this baby, so the earlier you start respecting me the better."

Kammron stopped laughing and stood up. He wiped the sweat from his forehead and lowered his eyes. He stepped to Shana and placed the tip of his nose against hers. "Bitch, put that muthafuckin' knife down, right now, or cut me wit' it," he ordered, with his nostrils flaring.

Shana placed the blade to the side of his throat. "Fuck that, I ain't putting shit down. You better respect me, Kammron. I may be young, but I'm the mother of your child, and I won't stand for you treating me like any other *thot* in them streets. You gon' give me my righteous do, or I'ma kill yo ass." She held the blade firmer to his throat.

Kammron smiled and tilted his head backward. "Do it bitch—do it! I muthafuckin' dare you, you ain't got the heart to." He strained his eyes to look down at her. "Bitch, if you gon' fuck wit' me you'll do it. I'm Killa Kamm, if you gon' fuck wit' me then you gon have to show me!" he hollered. "Do it!"

The knife shook inside of Shana's hand. She shook like crazy and held the blade. She didn't know if she could kill him. Didn't want the death of a human being on her conscious. She wasn't built like that. But at the same time, she felt deep in her soul that if she didn't kill him, one day he was going to kill her. She felt the nerve growing in her. Threw caution to the wind and was just about to slice his ass along his jugular, when Kammron knocked the knife from his neck.

"Bitch, stop playing. You ain't 'bout that graveyard shit. Stay in yo' lane. You finna have my shorty so I'ma give you a pass for that dumb shit you did. Don't do it no more. You understand me?"

Shana held the knife in her hand and looked up at him. "Kammron, you gon' respect me. I'm not finna be sitting around here getting my ass whooped by you on no daily basis. You can run that drag to them other hoes out there, but treat me like a Queen, because I am having your seed. Can you do that?"

Kammron shrugged his shoulders. "Shid, I don't know if I can, but I can very well try." He picked up the boxes of cereal, and placed them back on top of the refrigerator, then did the same with the bread.

Shana held the knife tighter. She had visions of rushing him and poking him up, but her nerve wasn't there. There was no way she could pull off such a heinous act. Instead, she dropped the knife in the sink and left out of the kitchen.

****

Showbiz cleared a line of raw and pulled his nose. He took a swallow from the bottle of Patron and wiped his mouth. Then he set the bottle on the table and looked across at Jimmy. Jimmy had two of Showbiz's shooters standing behind him with .50 Calibers in their hands, aimed at the back of his head. Showbiz sniffed and pulled his nose again.

"Word is out on you, Dunn. The island say you crossed, Diego and snuffed Stunna down in Jamaica. What you go to say about that?"

Jimmy separated his four lines, and took two hard, straight to the head. He closed his eyes as the poison took over his senses. Then laid his head back against the chair and smiled. "Yo', the Kid don't know what the fuck you even talking about. Somebody got their facts wrong."

Showbiz grunted, "I'm Showbiz muthafuckin' Vega, my facts are never wrong. You see I got the whole low down on yo' monkey ass. I know you knocked off, Stunna, so you could plug with his older brother, Flocka. Y'all want what the Vega family already has. I'm here to let you know that shit ain't happening, Kid.".

Jimmy responded, "If my facts are correct, and I know they are, then it's any day now for you Brooklyn niggas. It seems like y'all can't roll over on each other fast enough. That ain't my problem, Showbiz, it's yours." Jimmy felt the drug elevating him. His eyes were lower than a shiesty hustler on one twenty-fifth.

Showbiz slammed his hand on the table. "You Harlem niggas think y'all about to take over New York again, huh, muthafucka? Well, I'm here to let you know, I'd blow this bitch up before I let that happen. The Vega family owns New

York. Anybody that is opposing that is a threat. So, let me ask you a question, Jimmy. Are you a threat?"

Jimmy grabbed the bottle of Patron off the table and turned it up, guzzling. He downed a nice portion of the bottle and burped as loud as he could. He set the bottle back down. "If you deem another borough getting money in this city that has enough to go around, then you muthafuckin', right I'ma threat. I'm from Harlem, Kid. That's fast money, extravagant living, by any means necessary, balling out of muthafuckin' control ass borough. We get it however we gotta get it. That date all the way back before Malcolm X, who we called, Red, Kid." Jimmy slammed his hand on the table and mugged Showbiz. "Now if you tryna stop me from feeding my people, then yousa muthafuckin' threat."

Showbiz clenched his jaw and nodded his head. "Your father Ruiz has done great things for my father Vito back on the island. You have a certain level of protection provided because of your father, Ruiz. But if I report back to my old man that you are posing a threat to our financial security, and the stability of the family. I am sure he will lift the protection cloud from over you and Bonkers. If that happens, you do not want to find out what the Vega family is capable of. Now this is me coming to you as a friend of Havana, and an admirer of the Ponce family, get on ship with me and my people and I will ensure that you have no problem getting wealthy. Hell, you can even seek refuge in Brooklyn."

Jimmy frowned, stood up, and responded. "Nigga, I'm from Harlem. We stand alone! Always have, always will. Fuck Brooklyn, and every other borough that ain't Harlem USA. I couldn't give a muthafucka about no cloud of protection being over my head either. Here today gone tomorrow. The market is open, there are millions to be made. You better believe that Harlem finna make them muthafuckas." He mugged Showbiz. "I'm ready for whatever, nigga."

Showbiz leaned back in his chair and nodded his head. "Drop him back off at his mother's home. Do it now! Jimmy, you can bet yo' bottom dollar that we will be in touch. I'll see you soon."

"I look forward to it," Jimmy returned. He left out of the boardroom with Showbiz mugging the back of his head.

Chapter 12

Three weeks later, and Jimmy was seeing more birds than in an aviary. Flocka had kept his word and had the shipment of weight coming in by the boatload. Jimmy copped a warehouse right outside of Ruckers, that was once used as a public aid office for the people. It had cost him eighty thousand dollars, and he copped it under the guise of starting his own construction company, but construction was the furthest thing from his brain. Two weeks after he'd bought the building from the city, he had it detailed and flooded with hustlers from Harlem. Each floor held a different narcotic, and he assigned special men to be in place of each level. He held them solely responsible, and if anything was out of whack on that floor, he had intentions of wiping out the overseer for that level's entire family with no remorse. To him this shit was serious business, this was Harlem's chance to get back on the map in a major way with him at the gears. He could go down in Uptown's history as one of the greatest Kingpins to ever do it.

Not even a month in and he'd made a total of three million dollars in cash, of course, that wasn't much money, because half went back to Jamaica. After paying off his many workers, and security, he was left with a little less than a million to take home for himself which wasn't bad, but in New York was considered chump change. He couldn't be taken seriously by the other power players until he surpassed ten million, and he had his mind set on tripling that before the Winter came and ended. His first order of business was to fully conquer Harlem. In his opinion, there were too many low-level petty hustlers in the borough that were fuckin' up the major money from hitting his pockets. So, he decided to knock them off their small pedestals and make them come and work for him by promising to double their financial intake and giving them security when they roamed the streets.

There was just as many jackers, and robbers as there were hustlers in Harlem, and most dope boys were considered targets, and easy money, unless they worked under Jimmy. If this was the case, he would put them under his protections. They were able to be identified by the tattoo on their right shoulder of his picture. Yeah, it mighta been a bit extreme but in a good world like Harlem, anything that shielded you from the many predators was a blessing.

Of, course, there were the ones that refused to drop their own packs and fall under Jimmy's regime. For them, Jimmy had a solution. He hired a bunch of Jack boys from the borough who were incapable of doing anything but robbing. He put them on the payroll to specifically pull kick doors on the hustlers that refused to fall under his regime. He ordered them to treat them without mercy, and to strip them to the bone, even armed the Jackers and allowed them to keep anything they came up with all in the name of drug wars.

In six months, time, Harlem was fully under his control and the money was coming in by the bulk loads, so much so that Jimmy had seven accountants, and two financial advisors on his team. He began buying up the property in Harlem and oust the natives that ran restaurants and other local businesses. He bought out their leases, and loans fully took over their businesses and hired them to work for him. If they gave him any hassle or refused to cooperate most disappeared only to never be heard from again. In his mind, he was the biggest mobster Harlem had ever seen.

****

On April twenty seventh of twenty nineteen, Kammron Jr. was born into the world. He weighed in at seven pounds even and looked so much like Kammron it was scary. Kammron was holding him in his arms, bouncing him up and down, when Jimmy cruised through the door with a book bag over his shoulder. Kammron smiled at the sight of his, God brother.

"Yo', look at my seed, Dunn. My mans is in the building. He finally here," Kammron beamed. He was so excited he could barely think straight.

Jimmy walked over to him and motioned for Kammron to hand the baby over to him. "Let me see him, B. Let the God hold the new life." He took the book bag off his shoulder and handed it to Kammron. "This is for you."

Kammron handed off the baby and frowned. "Yo', what's this, Dunn?"

"Small token of my appreciation, and the welcoming of new life into Harlem. Check it out." He bounced Kammron Jr. up and down and rested his cheek against his.

Kammron stepped next to Shana and unzipped the book bag. He looked inside of it and pulled out two bricks of Peruvian flake. He placed them on Shana's lap carelessly, they were ducked taped and sealed. The rest of the book bag was filled with hundred-dollar bills totaling a hundred thousand dollars. Kammron shot a stare at him surprised. "Yo', Kid, what's all this?"

Jimmy continued to bounce Kammron Jr. "These kid's expensive son, you gon' find that out soon enough. You're already in the rear eighty-five hundred for birthing expenses, stuff just got real." Jimmy laughed.

Kammron finished brushing through the money. He placed the bricks back inside of the bag and zipped it up. "That's what's up, Kid, love."

Jimmy nodded. "You already know what it do."

Bonkers stepped into the room holding on to Yazzy's hand. Both father and daughter were fitted in purple and black Prada from head to toe. Bonkers had four iced gold ropes around his neck, and a matching Cartier watch with purple and black diamonds that glistened in the hospital room light.

Yazzy had three-carat purple diamonds in each ear and a necklace around her neck that was draped in purple diamonds. She had a diamond ring on each finger, and her hair fell past her shoulders now. She rushed to Kammron and hugged his legs. "Uncle!"

Kammron picked her up and planted kisses all over her beautiful face. "Hey, baby girl, you come here to see your new cousin?"

She nodded. "Yeah, Uncle Kamm, where is the baby? I wanna see it."

Jimmy kneeled down, and Yazzy hugged his neck, before her pure brown eyes set upon newborn, Kammron Jr. "Wow, what is it, a boy or a girl?"

Kammron laughed. "It's a boy, and his name is Junior."

Yazzy placed her small hand on Junior's chest. "Can I kiss him, Uncle Kamm?"

He nodded. "That's your cousin, you have to protect him. He loves you already, so you sure can."

Yazzy looked back at Bonkers for reassurance. After seeing him nod at her to move forward, she leaned and kissed Junior on the cheek. Then brought her head back and looked him over. "I'm going to protect you, Junior. You're my baby cousin!" She kissed him again.

Bonkers picked her up and held her in his arms. He strolled over to Shana. "How you holding up, Goddess?"

Shana was exhausted, her eyes drooped, and her body felt like it had been through hell. She shook her head. "My mouth dry, I need something to drink. I can barely swallow."

Kammron rushed to her side and gave her one of the hospital juices. "Yo', I can't believe Stacie ain't made it here yet. She said she would be here before you gave birth. That was an hour ago." He brushed her hair back and kissed her cheek.

Shana smiled, she felt so depleted. "It's okay, baby. Junior is here, he's safe and sound. That's all that matters." She drank the juice in a matter of seconds and closed her eyelids drifting off to sleep. The monitors in the background beeped and made all sorts of weird noises.

Jimmy placed his arm around Bonkers' neck. "Say, li'l' bruh, I got a move I need you and Kammron to buss at your earliest convenience. It involves a li'l' bloodshed, and fifty bands a piece for you two."

Bonkers handed Yazzy to Kammron and stepped into the hallway holding on to Jimmy's wrist. As soon as they entered the hallway they saw Stacie making her way down it. She was accompanied by Kammron's father. Bonkers already knew it was going to be trouble brewing ahead.

"Yo', Kid, I'm letting you know, right now we definitely want that move, so hold it to your chest. This fool Kammron's father walking up with Stacie, right now, I gotta put an end to this beef before it even starts, so hold on." He jogged off to meet Stacie right away.

Stacie saw him and smiled. "Hey, Bonkers." She had her hair down and was dressed in a nice Walmart dress that was full of colors. She looked young and effervescent.

Bonkers blocked her path. "Yo', Stacie, what you doing here with, Pops.? You know Kammron finna flip out when he see, Kid."

Stacie's warm smile turned into a frown. "Come on now, Bonkers, I ain't got time for no drama. I was at the ward visiting my mother when I ran into Kammron's father. While we were getting caught up, I got a call from Kammron telling me

Shana was going into labor. So, I told Pops what was taking place, and this man said he wanted to see his grandbaby. Who am I to prevent him from doing such a thing?"

Pops waved him off. "Boy, I don't need no permission to see my grandchild. Life is too short, and this is new life. Get yo' ass out of my way, now!"

Bonkers had the urge to stop him, but instead, he rushed into the room, and grabbed Yazzy from Kammron's arms, and moved the both of them out of the way. "Yo', Killa yo Pops outside wit' Stacie, whatever you do don't make a scene, Dunn."

Kammron's eyes got big, then small again. Before he could say what, he was feeling, Stacie came through the door and hugged his waist. "I'm sorry I'm late, baby, but that traffic was terrible. I brought somebody here with me, too. Let me see my grandbaby."

Kammron mugged the door in anticipation for the sight of his father, in whom his mother had always referred to as his sperm donor. From the corner of his eyes, he could see Jimmy hand Junior to Stacie. Shana was knocked out already, light beads of sweat peppered her forehead.

Pops came through the door and froze in his tracks. It was like he could feel Kammron's eyes burning holes into him. He held up his hands in submission. "Now, look Kamm, I ain't hear for none of that malarkey. I just wanna see my grandchild its first day out the womb," the dark-skinned, gray-eyed man assured him.

He and Kammron were mirror images for one another with the exception of Pops' dark-skin and slender build. Kammron was ripped, and muscular.

"Nigga, you ain't got no bidness being here. I don't know what you think finna happen, but you don't stand a chance in hell of being a part of my son's life. You wasn't even a part of mine old man."

Pops balled his hands into fists at his sides. "I didn't come here for all of this drama. I wanna see my baby. The mistakes I made with you ain't got nothing to do with him. I wanna do right by this one."

Kammron shook his head. "No, you don't muthafucka. You just heard how me and my boys moving and grooving through Harlem. You smell money, and you think Junior is going to be your way back into my life. B, you got the game fucked up, word to the borough man." Kammron walked in his direction.

Jimmy separated the two men. "Yo', Dunn, chill. Y'all can't do this stuff here, Kid. These white people have the police here faster than if a bank was being robbed."

"Yo', they gon' need to be, because if this old muthafucka don't get up out of here I'm about to put my foot up his abusive ass. This punk didn't even come to my mother's funeral man. Now he wanna flex like he care about my seed. Yo', my heart is an ice box to this fool man. Word to, Jehovah. Get yo ass outta here." Kammron pulled a Glock-9 from the small of his back and cocked it.

Yazzy screamed and buried her head into Bonkers armpits. "Get me out if here, Daddy, please. My Uncle finna get to shooting like my mama said he would."

Bonkers mugged Kammron and left the room with Yazzy in his arms. "Yo', Kid y'all need to squash that peace, Dunn. Y'all scaring my jewel and stuff. That's foul."

"Yeah, well in about five seconds I'm about to splash this clown. So, unless you want me to steal her innocence too you betta get baby girl up out of here," Kammron advised.

"You know what, fuck it, fuck it—I'll go. I don't need this shit, I just wanted to see my first born grandchild before I leave this earth, but you had to go this ugly, Kammron. That's typical you," Pops grumbled. He held himself up by the wall and hunched over with his eyes closed in pain.

Kammron mugged him. "Get yo ass out of here, Pops. Don't nobody want you here. Not me, not my son, or nobody else. Stacie, you brought this fool here. Give me my baby, and you take yo' ass back to the ward and drop him off. Next time before you make a decision, it'll be in your best interest to ask us it's okay before you bring somebody to one of our celebrations. You got me?"

Stacie was fuming, but she knew better than to argue with Kammron. His temper was ridiculous. So, instead of responding to him with a witty, classless remark, she decided to hold her silence. She handed him Junior and flared her nostrils. Then she kissed Shana on the forehead, and took hold of Pops' arm, leading him out of the room and down the hallway.

Kammron replaced his weapon and bounced Junior up and down. He looked into his son's handsome face. "It's okay, Junior, you ain't never gotta worry about me letting that filthy old man put his hands on you. Daddy got you, Kid. I'ma protect you to the best of my abilities. Word to, Jehovah, man."

Jimmy stood back with a smile on his face. As much as he and Kammron had butt heads over the years one thing he had to admire was how cold-blooded the man was. Kammron didn't give two fucks about anybody outside of his circle, and for those inside his circle, he was willing to go to hell and back for. When it came down to a man in Jimmy's position, Kammron was exactly the kind of man he needed working under him. He knew it was in his best interest to keep him closer than his shadow.

Chapter 13
Newark, New Jersey

Bonkers adjusted his Prada tuxedo and pulled back his left sleeve to show off his gold Rolex watch that was sprinkled in white diamonds. He sprayed on a smidgen of Prada cool water cologne and picked a piece of lint off his pant leg.

He stood back and looked himself over in the full-length mirror. "Yo', that's a good looking man, right there. Word up."

Kammron came and butted him out of the way. He stood before the full-length mirror dressed in a black and white Burberry Tuxedo, over Prada loafers. He pulled back his left sleeve and turned his wrist from side to side so he could watch the frosted Rolex twinkle in the light.

"Say, Kid, we can't lie having money just fits us. Look how we looking, I mean especially me. I make all of this shit look better than them mafuckin' models that be on the runways and what not." He cheesed, and ran his finger across his teeth, then stood back and looked over his reflection. "Bonkers, all this time we thought we was balling and shit, Kid when we wasn't. I don't give a fuck who you are, if you ain't hot then you ain't doing shit. I got sixty gees in each ear lobe. Fifty gees on my wrist, and a hundred fifty thousand around my neck. Harlem most definitely in the muthafuckin' building."

Bonkers bumped him back out of the way. "Yo', nigga you ain't the only one styling. This that a hundred and forty fifth and Broadway shit, right here, Harlem world. I'm ready to flex on any major nigga with no remorse. These Jersey niggas ain't finna be seeing us Kid, word up."

Kammron placed both Glocks in their holsters and pulled his tuxedo coat over them. He frowned his face. "I hate these Jersey niggas Bonkers. All these clowns be acting like they harder than the apple son. My word, anytime we gotta do bid-ness out here I swear that shit just irks my nerves." Kammron tossed a breath strip into his mouth and closed it. The cool mint dissolved and freshened his breath.

Bonkers loaded up his weapons. "You know how the game go. In order for Harlem to take over the world, we gotta venture out to all areas. Besides, we can both use another fifty gees a piece, and Jimmy wants us to act as his ambassadors. Our job is to get in and get out of here as soon as possible. It's as simple as that. Let's rollout, Kid." Bonkers took one more look at himself in the mirror and gave himself a stamp of approval.

Kammron once again moved him out of the way and smiled while looking himself over. "Damn that's a handsome nigga, right there. Bitches finna be trying to have my baby Son word up. But I ain't doing it, though, Junior already costing me a fortune." He lowered his head and shook it, at that reality.

Bonkers came and placed his hand on his shoulder. "Man, ain't nobody says providing for a family was going to be easy. This shit takes hard work, and dedication."

Kammron moved from under his hand and backed away. "Whoa, whoa, whoa, Dunn quit talking that family shit. I ain't with that, me and Shana just have a son together. I'm nineteen, Boss, a family is the furthest thing from my mind." He felt angry even thinking about the prospect of being in a family with any female.

Kammron didn't like restrictions of any kind. He loved Junior and would go to the ends of the earth for him, but when it came to his mother he respected, and cared about her to a certain extent. He still wanted to be free to roam.

Bonkers laughed and shook his head. "You're still the same old, Kammron. Nigga, you might never change. Come on, let's go and make this deal for, big bruh, so we can get back to the Apple."

****

Jimmy popped the cork on the bottle of Moët and allowed the fizz to bubble over his fingers, as the small Yacht bounced up and down over the waves of the water. The sun was shining bright in the sky, he protected his eyes by use of a pair of Cartier sunglasses that ran him five gees. His long hair blew in the wind behind him. Two thick ass Jamaicans continued to slow wind in front of his face naked. They held their hands up in the air and only moved the lower portion of their body. Their juicy booties jiggled along with their thighs. Jimmy smacked one on the ass and squeezed her cheek. She moaned, and bent all the way over, spreading her thighs, exposing the cleft between. Jimmy took the champagne and poured the liquid at the top of her crack, held his mouth at the bottom of her pussy, and drank it as it dripped from her gap, slurping loudly. She moaned and closed her eyes together. The other Jamaican Queen, pulled on her own nipples, aroused at the sight of the two of them. She rubbed in between the other female's legs and opened her pussy so the champagne could give her tingles as it traveled through her split.

Jimmy looked up. "Say, Ma, bring ya ass over here and get me right." He unzipped his Gucci jeans, pulled his piece out, stroked it a few times, and leaned back.

The second Jamaican pulled her fingers from between her friend's thighs and kneeled in front of him. She stroked his pipe, kissed the head, twirled her tongue around it over and over, before sucking him into her mouth, and giving him some of the best head of his life, while her friend squatted over the back of the couch, and his face, and rode it to a strong climax.

****

Bonkers was trying his best to remain calm, but his blood was boiling, as he sat in the small room that seemed to have poor ventilation. There was a red, light bulb screwed in that helped them to see a little bit, but not nearly as much as he wanted too. Damien had two bodyguards standing behind his chair, with mugs on their faces. Bonkers eyed them closely, he didn't like the way Damien the Jamaican was talking to him, and Kammron as if they were nothing more than peasants. He pushed the plate of Tar to the side and looked across the table at the dark-faced man, whose eyes were so red they looked like he'd been crying for a year straight.

Damien inhaled a thick cloud of Ganja and blew the smoke across the table into Kammron's direction. "So, dats me proposal, right there. If Jimmy wants to use my fishing docks as a place for importing, then he's going to have to pay me fifteen percent of all imports and accept my tariff of fifty gees a month. If he can't accept that, he's going to have to go another route. It's as simple as that." Damien took a pull from the blunt and dumped the ashes from the cigar into the ashtray. Once again, he blew his smoke into Kammron's direction. He didn't like the way the young man mugged him. It was Damien's way of trying to provoke him to do anything stupid so he could slay him.

Kammron closed his eyes and opened them with a mug on his face. "Jimmy said he's willing to pay you fifty gees a month period for use of your docks. The fee ain't going no higher. It's either you gon' take this scratch, or ain't shit moving. It's as simple as that. So, what are you going to do Damien the Jamaican?"

Damien sat back in his chair and broke out laughing. Remnants of smoke drifted from his nostrils. He scratched his scruffy beard and cleared his throat. "So, you think you can bring your ass all the way from New York and tell me what to do with my docks out here in New Jersey. You really think that is going to fly, my boy?" he asked Kammron, and looked back from him to Bonkers, then back to Kammron before busting out laughing.

Bonkers felt the sweat pour down his back. His trigger finger was itching. He felt frantic and angrier then he had been in a long time. He never took kindly to underestimation, and he seriously felt it was exactly how Damien was treating them as if they were not a threat. Jimmy told them to use murder as the last case scenario because he needed Damien's docks to import his goods from the islands. The ones in New York we're currently spoken for by the bosses from the Islands, and those back in Sicily. He didn't have enough clout, nor people in his pocket to be able to use them. New Jersey was cheaper, and only under the control of Damien the Jamaican. He wanted to use Jersey as an importing, and deporting post until he got his money right, then he could jockey for position with the harbor back in New York.

Kammron took a deep breath and placed a smile on his face. "Check this out, Damien. We're all businessmen here. We think fifty thousand dollars is more than enough money to show our gratitude each month. Now we're not saying that it's going to be the final number, but a start. Once things start to flow well for a few months, I am sure Jimmy will have no problem upping the payment, but we have to crawl before we walk."

Damien grunted, and snatched the Crown Royal from the table, pouring himself a glass of the brown liquor and downing it. "Fifty thousand ain't enough to wipe my ass with. You think I'ma 'bout to let you filthy New Yorkers utilize my city, and my waters so you can transport shit back and forth and make a killing while you pay me peanuts? Do you really think I'm that stupid?" He felt his temper rising. "I got broke mutha-fuckas hitting me up on a daily basis and offering he more than fifty gees to allow them to do less than what you're proposing. You need to tell, Jimmy, I said come with the big numbers, or kiss my muthafuckin ass! I'm not, Diego, he ain't gon' strong arm me like some pussy. You got that?" He stood up. "Now get the fuck out of my city, both of you."

Kammron sat there with a smile on his face. "Yo', I thought we were invited to the five-star soiree tonight. What because of this li'l' misunderstanding we're no longer wel-come?"

"Get the fuck out, right now!" Damien hollered.

Bonkers mugged the man and nodded his head. "A'ight then, you fellas have a good day. We'll be sure to send your message to, Jimmy. Come on, Dunn!"

****

Jimmy paced back and forth in front of Kammron, and Bonkers. He balled his fists and bit into his bottom lip. "Yo', you mean to tell me that was that fool's response? He told me to kiss his ass, no bullshit?"

Kammron rested his Flocks in the table, pulled the platter of North Korean over to him and took two lines straight to the head. He pinched his nostrils together and tilted his head back. The high took over him, right away. He closed his eyes with a smile on his face. "That's exactly what that ma'fucka said, Kid. Yo', it took every ounce of will power I had to not blast his ass, but your orders were for us to only move that way as a last resort."

Jimmy sighed. "Yo', I gotta touch bases with, Flocka. That fool Damien got a lot of love from a few of the major Rastas on the island. I would have y'all ass hit him right away so we could move into that part of Newark that we need, but this shit is a process. That's just the way the game goes."

Bonkers sat back and kicked his feet up on the table. He was Facetiming with Yazzy. She was trying to show him the new doll Yasmin had bought for her.

"Damn, Bonkers, can you please pay attention to what the fuck we got going on, right now? This muthafucka is holding up our operation and impeding on us making more two million dollars a week. Now we gon' need to fix this problem like asap, I'ma make a few calls, and y'all get ready to roll back out to Newark."

Kammron wiped his face with his right hand and smacked his lips. He was on cloud nine already. "Yo', Son, I don't like them Jersey dudes man. It seem like every time we go out there it's always some bullshit involved. I'm letting you know right now that the next time I roll out that way it's gon' be a serious problem. Tired of playing with cats out that way period."

Bonkers blew kisses at Yazzy and put his phone away. He looked up to Jimmy and saw he was mugging him. "What's good, nigga? Why you looking at me like that?"

Jimmy flared his nostrils. "How nice of you for joining us."

Kammron snickered. "Yasmin got that nigga pussy whip, Kid, word up. Ever since bruh been rocking wit' her he been acting some type of way."

"Yasmin, ain't got me shit, nigga, I'm good. For the record, I was Facetiming with my daughter, but you, niggas don't need to worry about that. What's up next on the agenda?" Bonkers asked, irritated.

Kammron laughed and covered his head as if Bonkers was getting ready to throw a blow. "Jimmy leave him alone, Son about to blow," he quipped.

Jimmy glared at Kammron. "Look y'all, this shit is serious. It ain't a game. We could either gain millions in all of this, or we can lose money, but like I said I'm finna holler at Flocka and see if I can go ahead with this move. Y'all just get ready to go out there no matter what. Kammron, I heard you loud and clear. Trust and believe if I give you the go ahead and send you back to Newark that mean you're supposed to do you. You feel me?"

Kammron closed his eyes and dozed on and off. He opened his eyelids that pained him to keep open and slurred. "Long as you know what's good, that's all that matters."

Bonkers pulled his nose and sat back in his hair. He was feeling a bit annoyed at how they had come down on him for spending digital time with his daughter. He wanted to buss the move and get it over with. That way he could chill inside the crib with Yasmin, and Yazzy. For him, family time was extremely therapeutic.

"Yo', let's get this shit over with so we can take some time off. I need a few weeks to myself."

Kammron popped his eyes open and looked him over. "Yo', you taking that shit personal? We was just fuckin' wit' you. Damn, nigga don't be getting all soft on me and shit."

"I said what I said. We gon' handle this bidness, then I need a li'l' time off, that's just that," Bonkers stated, before leaving out of the room.

Kammron shook his head irritated, and once again a deep hatred for Yasmin washed over him. "Yeah, a'ight, Dunn walk off then.

Chapter 14

It took three additional weeks before Jimmy was given the go-ahead on Damien the Jamaican. His death would come at a price. In order for Jimmy to knock him out of the game he was charged a significant fee of one million dollars, and it had to be paid upfront to Flocka. Then Flocka would send half of the money to his father's associates that were overseers of the island. When it came to the game anything a man did, he had to get permission, and the right palms had to be greased.

Kammron slid the black leather gloves on his hands and wiggled his fingers while pulling them back. Next came to the Freddie Krueger mask. He looked over at Bonkers as he fastened the Jason mask across his face. "Son, you been mad quiet over there. You good?"

Bonkers sighed and fixed the mask on his face. "Yazzy, sick with the flu. I can't get her off my brain bruh no matter how hard I try. Now we about to go in here and run this whole crib, waste kids and all. Man, sometimes the price of becoming Dons is just too much for me." He cocked his .45 and placed it in the small of his back. Then made sure the knives were properly placed inside his fatigue jacket and felt his adrenalin kick in. "Let's go do this shit." He grabbed the door handle, ready to jump out of the Buick Lacrosse they'd stolen for the hit.

Kammron grabbed a hold of his arm. "Wait a minute, bruh, I can tell somethin' ain't right. You seem like you falling off from all this shit. Fucks the problem?"

It was one o'clock in the morning, and it had just started to rain. There was a light breeze coming from the south that caused the car to sway a bit. Lightning made its appearance in the sky. The thunder growled, just before the rain picked up harder.

Bonkers pulled off his mask. "Yo', I don't wanna talk about that shit, Kid. Right now, my mind's just all fucked up. Ever since Yazzy came back into my life dawg all I can think about is her and her mother. I know I'm only nineteen, but I'm starting to think about that family shit more and more. This street shit is still in me, but so is that family shit, Kid. My word, I just wanna make a few million, and fall back."

Kammron was fuming, he felt like his right-hand man was flipping on him. For as long as he'd been in the streets Bonkers had been right beside him doing just as much dirt as he was. To imagine him leaving him behind to go and layup with a family was enough to drive Kammron crazy. "Fall back to do what?"

Bonkers shrugged his shoulders. "I don't know, to take care of my li'l' family, bruh. I gotta be a man for them. If not me, then who?"

Kammron was seething. Now more than ever he was ready to get rid of Yasmin, and even Yazzy if he had too. He refused to lose his right-hand man under any circumstances. "Yo', let's gon' head and handle this bidness. We'll talk about this other shit a li'l' later." He opened the door and stepped into the night. The only thing on his mind was getting finish with their task at hand so he could find a way to get rid of Yasmin, and Yazzy. He felt if they were gone, he could have his right-hand man back.

Bonkers jogged to catch up with him just as Kammron made his way into the alley. "Yo', hold ya ass up, nigga. I still gotta send this text so they can move they ass around." He was texting away as he walked up to him.

Kammron was in his own zone, he felt murderous. He eased into the back gate, and two Jamaicans jumped from the side of the garage with machetes in their hands. Kammron upped his gun, ready to buss.

"Whoa, whoa, whoa. We got the go-ahead, my man. We from New York," Bonkers said, trying to lighten the situation.

One of the Jamaicans looked the masked two over. He was just about to raise the machete and go crazy when his phone vibrated, and a text came through ordering him to allow the wolves to pass. He looked from the phone to them, and backed into the shadows, pulling the other Jamaican along with him.

Bonkers took that as a sign for them to proceed forward. He waved for Kammron to follow him. They jogged to the back of the house, located the cellar that was promised to be opened, and slipped inside of it after pulling the doors open, and closing them back.

The basement smelled stale and felt swampy. Both men marched over the concrete and headed to the stairs. Once up then, Kammron eased open the door and stepped into the kitchen. The house was pitch black. It smelled of incense. Off in the distance, there was the light from the television. Bonkers nodded at Kammron and pointed in that direction. Kammron pointed toward the top of the stairs, indicating that he would look for Damien up there.

Kammron leaned into Bonkers. "Remember, Jimmy said he wants the whole house slaughtered, there are no exceptions."

"Yo', I got it, I'll meet you upstairs," Bonkers assured him, as he tiptoed toward the living room where the television was playing. He pulled the .45 from his waistband and screwed in the silencer. He crouched low and made his way there. When he got, ten steps from actually entering the room, he held his breath and zoomed in.

There was Damien's brother sitting on the couch drunk as a skunk. On his lap was an AK-47, cocked and loaded. The man looked up at the television screen as the late-night Olympic tryouts for the hundred-yard dash played across the screen.

"Come on now, Shelly-Ann, dis is yer year to bring home da gold to Jamaica. Tired of dee Americans taking what's ours." He leaned his head, and tooted a line of coke hard, then fell back on the couch as the bout started.

Bonkers made sure the silencer was as tight as it possibly could be. He kneeled down, and closed one eye, aiming with the best of his abilities, slowly scooting forward foot by foot.

"Go, go, go, you silly, gal. Run, run, run, yes, yes, yes!" He scooted to the edge of the couch and threw his fists in the air as Shelly-Ann crossed the finish line first. He grabbed the beer from the tabletop and began to swallow it in large gulps.

Bonkers, bit into his bottom lip and smiled before firing back to back to back. "Muthafucka."

Damien's brother felt the first slug enter into his jaw. It burned through his skin and knocked a hole in his face shattering six teeth. Blood began to pour from the intrusion. The next slug punched a hole in his neck and removed a large portion of his vocal cord. The man choked on his saliva and blood. The third and fourth slug knocked the back of his head off and spun him around in the couch before he fell sideways to his death.

Bonkers rushed to his side and placed his ear to the man's nostrils. He waited to see if he could hear any intake of breath when he heard none, he grabbed the AK from the floor and stood up.

****

Kammron crept down the hallway and stopped outside of Damien's bedroom door. He slowly twisted the knob and eased it open. The sound of the sleeping Damien was apparent, the man snored like a bear during hibernation season. He eased the Kitana blade out if its holster, and tiptoed toward the sleeping man, in the side of him was a fourteen-year-old Jamaican girl that the mobster had brought over from the island as a sex slave. Kammron didn't know Jimmy had the entire set up of Damien, but he was glad he did because it made, he and Bonkers' jobs that much easier. Kammron tiptoed to the bed, and an evil smile spread across his face. He mugged Damien. He tried to remember the feeling he'd had three weeks ago as they were sitting in front of the man and he made it seem as if they were nothing more than peasants. Kammron reached and smacked him as hard as he could.

"Wake yo' bitch ass up," he hissed.

Damien jerked out of his sleep and sat up, barely lucid. There was a crazy stinging from the slap. His eyes struggled to focus in on the Freddy Krueger mask in front of him. Before he could utter a word, he felt the blade enter into his throat. He tried to scream but the steel cut him off. The blade was ripped out of his neck and slammed into his right cheek. It cut through his sinuses. Blood gushed out of him. He prayed it was a nightmare, but the man was too real. He jerked on the bed as the blade was used to penetrate him over and over again.

Kammron left him twisted, pulled the silenced gun from his waist and fired four slugs into the sleeping girl with no remorse. The silk sheets turned bloody red and matted to their bodies. He left out of the room with it smelling like gunpowder and incense.

****

Bonkers found the five-gallon gas can in the basement and traveled through the entire house pouring the liquid all over the floors. As soon as Kammron was back at his side, he pulled

125

the lighter from his pocket. "Yo', you left the other three bound upstairs?"

Kammron nodded. "Yeah, that's everybody. Spark that shit and let's get up out of here. This shit is a don' dotta." He rushed to the backdoor and opened it after turning the eyes of the stove on.

Bonkers lit the flame, and the house ignited in a fiery blaze. Both men took off running out of the backdoor, and toward the alley. The two Jamaicans from earlier stood in the backyard looking at the house. Kammron and Bonkers ran past them.

Part way to the alley, Kammron stopped, and upped both, .45s. "Say Jamaica!" Both men turned around to see what Kammron wanted. Before they could turn all the way around, Kammron's guns was jumping in his hands slug after slug. He filled the men with hole after hole until they fell in the grass, slain. Kammron jogged over to them and felt their necks to make sure there was no longer a pulse. After confirming that there was not, he took off running behind Bonkers with his guns smoking.

Chapter 15

After the pair knocked Damien out of the way, Jimmy was free to expand his imports. Flocka finally felt secure enough to send Jimmy a heavy shipment without worrying if it would get to him by plane, or if the hangars were being watched by the Feds. Now he could communicate the hustle to him through the use of boats. In only three months Jimmy's profits had increased from a mere million dollars a week, to three million, that was enough to feed the animals in Harlem, and grease the right palms. Through the borough, he was finally able to move about like a true Don was supposed to. The residents of Harlem referred to him as the Capo or the Don. He felt powerful, he felt like New York was finally his for the taking.

A week after he deposited his first five million dollars into an offshore account, Flocka sent for him and told him he wanted to spend some time with him out in Dubai. That was right up Jimmy's alley. He'd heard so many great things about Dubai that he couldn't wait to fly out so he could have a good time. So, he packed a suitcase with some of his best jewelry, and a few outfits, and headed to the airport where there was a first-class ticket waiting for him.

****

Kammron drank from the Budweiser and eyed Yasmin from across the backyard through his Dolcé and Gabbana sunglasses. Her tight-fitting skirt clung to her curves more than usual. She looked like she'd put on at least ten pounds since she'd come back to Harlem. The weight looked good on her. She grabbed a plate of baby back ribs and handed them to a curvy female that looked like she was happy to get it. Yasmin sashayed back across the backyard playing hostess. The sight of her both aroused, and angered Kammron. He kept his arm around Shana's neck, but his focus was all Yasmin.

"Baby, you okay?" Shana asked noticing Kammron had been quiet for nearly ten minutes. That was unlike him, he was always saying something or getting up to mess with Bonkers at the very least, but he'd been acting extremely strange for the last few days.

Kammron yawned and stretched his hands over his head. "Yeah, I'm good. This sun getting to me a li'l bit, but other than that I'm one hunnit. What's good with you?"

She pulled the top of the stroller over Junior to block him from the rays of the sun. "I was just checking on you, baby, that's all. It ain't like you to be so quiet."

Kammron watched Yasmin bend over. Her tight skirt rose above her thighs and showcased the bottom of her ass cheeks that were encased in a pair of red lace boy shorts. His penis throbbed over and over. "Like I said this heat getting the better of me, that's all. I'm good though." He watched Yasmin walked over to them with two plates filled to the max in her hands. The closer she got the more she both excited and pissed him off.

"Here y'all go, I hope y'all are enjoying our li'l barbecue. This was my way of breaking in the new house." She leaned over to place both plates on the table. Her perfume attacked Kammron's nostrils. It sent chills up and down his spine and drove him crazy.

"Girl, I'm starving, all Junior wanna do is feed all day long. He be having me all kinds of hungry. Oh, and the party is cracking, thank you for inviting us." She picked up her fork and said a prayer over her food.

Yasmin smiled at Kammron. "How about you, Kammron. Are you having a good time?" She popped back on her legs and looked into his brown eyes.

He smirked. "It's alright, I mean y'all could play a li'l bit more of that Harlem music. But for what it is it's cool."

Yasmin laughed. "Boy, you ain't never satisfied. It don't matter if we had a circus jumping off in here, you still wouldn't be happy. Enjoy the food." She stepped away with her ass jiggling like jello. The skirt couldn't help but raise up on to her waist. She'd left behind a scent of Prada.

Kammron sucked his teeth, grabbed his plate of food, and set it on his lap. After seeing Yasmin in the new light, he'd made up his mind, he was going to get him some of that pussy no matter what.

Bonkers came across the backyard holding Yazzy in his arms. He sat her down and shook up with Kammron. "What's the move, Kid?"

Kammron gave him a half hug and looked over his shoulder at Yasmin as she bent over again. This time it looked like the skirt rose higher. He felt like she was deliberately teasing him, though in actuality she didn't have a clue as to what was going through his mind. She only tolerated Kammron as much as she possibly could because of Bonkers. If it were up to her, they would never come in contact with him ever again.

"Yo', I'm good, Boss. Sitting here enjoying this good sunshine, and about to tear into this here barbecue." He sat back down and forked up a portion of Potato salad that was made just right.

Bonkers scanned the get-together. There were seven other couples present. People he barely knew, they were Yasmin's friends, each couple had a child around the same age as Yazzy. He didn't care, as long as his girls were having a good time, he was straight.

"Yo', Kid, I got two-floor seats to the Knicks game tomorrow night. They taking on the Rockets, we gon' get to see the home team put a li'l' work in. What's good, you fuckin' around?"

"You already know I'll be there. I need to kick back and be on some manly shit for a few days. I been doing the father thing with her for a month straight. I feel like I'm losing my mind a somethin'."

Shana smacked her lips and frowned. "Damn, Killa, you coulda at least waited until y'all walked off or something, rude." She rolled her eyes.

"Man, shut yo' ass up, I said what the fuck I said. Don't be interrupting me when I'm talking to my mans and shit either. Stay in yo lane."

Shana turned back around and shut up. She didn't want to get Kammron's temper flaring. He'd been cool for the past week. She knew it was about time for him to act up. She still did not have the energy to fight with him and felt to respond to his verbal assaults would have been a waste of time. So, she sat in silence, stewing on the inside.

"Yo', see what I'm saying, Kid. I need to get the fuck away for a minute. In addition to that game, how about we go to a strip club? See some hoes a somethin'?"

Yasmin walked up and placed her hand on Bonkers' shoulder. "Uh-uh, Kammron, don't be talking that negative jazz to my man. He don't need to go to no strip club. We already have a pole in our bedroom, I'm all the stripper this one here need. Ain't that right baby?" She kissed Bonkers' cheek.

Kammron mugged her, feeling like he was ready to blow. He balled his fists together and clenched his teeth. Had he not been wearing the shades Yasmin would have seen how evil he looked, and it would have spooked her.

Bonkers smiled weakly and took Yasmin's hand from his shoulder. ''Hold fast, baby, let me holla at my man's real quick. It's clear he's goin' through somethin'." Bonkers could sense the tension in the air. Even though he wanted to be lovey-dovey with Yasmin he didn't feel now was the right time.

Yasmin felt offended. She took a step back and grunted. "Well, okay then, I guess that's my fault. Maybe you do need to go out to the strip club with him." She rolled her eyes and stormed off. Bonkers tried to grab her, but she knocked his hand away and kept walking.

Kammron stood next to him. "Damn, Kid, what is it all of these hoes time of the month or somethin'?"

Bonkers watched Yasmin continue to play hostess. He felt horrible. He knew he needed to say something positive to her, but it would have to wait. She was steaming, and he knew it. One of the things he always wanted to prevent was having a public argument. Nothing good came from those. In his opinion it only caused both parties to do more than they should.

Shana stood up. "Kammron, I'm ready to go. Can you take me home?"

Kammron frowned. "Yo', sit yo' ass down until I'm ready to go. Can't you see I'm still hollering at my mans, right now?"

Junior woke up and began to cry, softly at first, then he was having a full-blown tantrum. His diaper was wet, and he was starving for some of Shana's breast milk.

Shana pushed the stroller forward, and back again. "Come on, Kammron. He done already used up all of his Pampers here, and I'm not about to let him sit in his filth. Plus, he's hungry! I can't feed him in front of everybody, now can I?"

Kammron was irritated. Junior's screaming, and now Shana was getting on his nerves. He was seconds away from snapping out. "Shorty, I'll be ready to go in a minute, damn!"

Shana rolled her eyes and sat back down in her chair. "Kammron, you know how quick he gets rashes. That's all I'm saying." She picked him up out of the stroller and sure enough, he had soiled his diaper. His stomach was also growling.

"Yo', Kid, maybe you should gon' head and drop them off. I'll fuck wit' you later," Bonkers encouraged him.

Kammron shot daggers at him. "Damn, nigga, now you tryna tell me what to do, too?"

Bonkers shook his head. "N'all Dunn, whatever you do is on you."

Junior screamed louder, now he had nearly the whole party looking in their direction. This annoyed Kammron. He was so irritated he was shaking.

Yasmin came over and popped back on her legs. Kammron caught the way her ass jiggled in the skirt, and it did something to him once again. "Girl, if they still wanna talk I'll drop you off real quick, besides I can use a good female to female conversation anyway. That cool with you?"

Shana nodded. "That would be a blessing. That way I can give him a quick bath and feed his little gut before I put him back to bed." She sat the screaming Junior back into his stroller and fastened him in. She had never been angrier in her entire life.

Yasmin turned to Bonkers. "Baby, you don't mind if I take the Durango, and drive her home, do you? The party is clearing out, and she really should get this baby home, besides I gotta stop at the salon and get my laptop anyway."

Bonkers shook his head. "N'all, gon' head, I'ma keep Yazzy here with me, though. She wanna watch a few movies once the party is over so that's what we'll be doing until you get back."

Yasmin kissed him on the cheek. "Alright, that's cool. I'll see you in a little while. I definitely need me some girl talk." She laughed and rubbed Shana's back. "You ready to go girl?"

Shana didn't dare make eye contact with Kammron from fear of what he might say or do. "Yeah, I'm ready." She pushed the stroller out if the backyard with her heart beating in her chest.

Kammron clenched his jaw until they were out of the backyard, and on about their business. His nostrils flared. "Yo', I don't know how you do that shit all day everyday man. I just ain't built to be up under no bitch for the long haul. This family life is weak to me, Bonkers, word up." He made his way into the house.

Bonkers followed behind him and met back up with him in the kitchen, where he saw Kammron grab another brew out of his refrigerator. Kammron slammed the door, and they could hear the glass on the inside tink into one another. "Yo', calm yo ass down nigga before you break my shit in there."

Kammron lowered his head. "My fault, bruh, I'm just stressing, that's all. On some real shit, I need a guy's night out. We need to go to the game. Hit up a strip club and go somewhere else. Shid, I wish we could fly out to Vegas for the weekend, but I know Yasmin a put her li'l toes all up yo ass if you even tried anything like that. Wouldn't she?" Kammron was trying to patronize him.

Bonkers waved him off. "N'all, I'll holler at her and see what she say."

That was the wrong response. Kammron was hoping Bonkers fell back into his old self and snapped about a bitch having so much say so over him, but instead he was humble and mature. It was sickening to him.

"Yo', Shorty got yo ass locked down, Kid. Since when you need permission to do anything?" Kammron asked walking into the living room, sitting down.

Bonkers followed him. "Since Yazzy was found out to be my daughter, and Yasmin is her mother. Like I said before I gotta do right by them, Killa. I'm all they have. I'm still ya boy, and I'm still fucking wit' you the long way, but I got a family now. Nah, mean?"

"Yeah, nigga, I get it. Damn, you ain't gotta keep throwing that shit in my face. Every time we're supposed to do something like we used to do, and you snub me for them I'm reminded you got a family."

Bonkers sat across from him. "Bruh, you got a family, too. It ain't like I'm the only one. Maybe you should take some time to get to know Shana and Junior for that matter. You'd be surprised how happy they could make you once you embrace the fact that they are under your domain."

Kammron jerked his head back. "My what?"

"Your domain, Kid. That's basically saying they were destined to be under your protection. They were put there by Jehovah man. Our creator."

Kammron pulled his glasses from his face and eyed him closely. "Nigga, what the fuck is you even talking about?"

"Kid, Yasmin, been having me listening to these sermons that break down the household, and the responsibility of the man. Yo', they blow my mind every time I listen to them. You see we're Adam's kids. We each have our own gardens that God places us in as men. After he sees we are ready to actually be men, he blesses us with a woman, and our children. We as men are responsible for both, it's called your domain. There's a verse in the Bible that says any man that doesn't provide for and protects those under his domain, or in his household will be rejected by Jehovah man. That's like one of the worst sins. We as men have to—"

Kammron slammed his hands on the table and stood up. "Nigga, I don't give no fuck about that shit you been listening to or reading. Fuck them sermons," he spat and wiped his mouth. "And second of all she's not my wife or my woman, she's Junior's mother, nothing more, nothing less. Kid, you can kick that drag to somebody else cause I ain't feeling it. I gotta use the bathroom." Kammron stood up and left the room.

Bonkers watched him disappear, he lowered his head and shook it. The more and more conversations he and Kammron had the more he was really starting to understand the two were growing apart.

Chapter 16

Shana took the Kleenex from the box on the table in front of her and dried her eyes. She'd finally gotten Junior off to sleep, and now it was as if there were a ball of emotions flooding her all at once. She scooted back on the couch and crossed her thick thighs.

Yasmin came and sat next to her. She rested her hand on Shana's knee. "Girl, you shouldn't be giving this man your tears. You have to be strong, if not for yourself, then for Junior. You owe him that strength.

More tears fell from Shana's eyes. She shook her head and sniffled. "I'm just so tired, Yasmin. This man has a hold on me like none other. I'm losing my mind as well as weight. I just don't know what to do." She lowered her head all the way to her lap and broke down.

Yasmin rubbed her back, she felt so sympathetic. She could only imagine what being in a relationship with somebody like Kammron could've been like. She knew he was crazy, egotistical, and extremely unstable. The fact that Shana had a baby by him had to make her feel trapped.

She leaned her forehead against Shana's. "Girl, I hope you know I'm here for you, right? Anything you need from me, anything you need me to do, I'm here. One hundred percent. You do not have to travel through this valley alone. Okay?"

Shana continued to cry. She felt both weak, and afraid. There were so many thoughts running through her mind that she had to open up to Yasmin to let her know some of them, especially the major one. Even though she didn't know if she could fully trust her or not, she still had to tell somebody. "Yasmin, can I tell you something?"

Yasmin nodded and continued to rub her back. "Yeah, my sista, you can tell me anything."

Shana shook her head and squeezed ears out of her eyes. "No, girl, I mean can I tell you something heavy. Something I need you to swear you will never tell anybody else because it's that serious." She straightened up and faced her. "Can I tell you something like that, and you'll promise me it will never leave this room?"

Yasmin's antennas went on high alert. She didn't know if she wanted to know any secrets. She didn't have a clue what secret Shana could be holding but being involved with Kammron she could only imagine. "Girl, you know what I don't wanna know 'bout nothing I shouldn't know about. Especially if it got anything to do with Kammron. That's y'all business. Now if it is something to do with just you, then sure I would love to know what is bothering you."

Shana remained silent, and once again dropped her head. "That's okay, then. Anyway, I appreciate you being here. There's no telling how long he woulda made me stay at that party."

Yasmin stood up. "Yeah, girl, don't mention it. But anyway, I betta be getting back. I gotta stop at my office and pick up my laptop so I can go over the books for our three shops. I'm behind, right now. Make sure you hit me up on Facebook later on tonight when you get your mind right." She made her way toward the front door and took a hold of the handle when Shana stood up.

"Yasmin, he killed my sister, Shelly. He killed her, and I don't know what to do," she cried dropping to her knees sobbing. Snot ran out of her nose as she rocked back and forth.

Yasmin was stuck in place, she closed her eyes, and sighed. Then turned around and looked the sobbing Shana over. "Girl, how do you know?" She walked back to her and kneeled down, resting her hand on her back.

Shana began to shake, she felt she'd made a big mistake by letting out such a major secret, but it was driving her crazy. She needed somebody else to know about it. Needed advice on what she should do. She felt so stuck, so powerless, and guilty each time she laid in the bed with Kammron knowing what he'd done to Shelly.

"Did you hear me, girl? How you know, he killed your sister?" Yasmin wondered if she'd seen it take place, and if she had she wanted to ask her what role Bonkers took part in the deadly debacle.

"Kammron was hopped up on liquor, and dope one night, and he admitted everything. He was going to take my life as well. We fought, and I wound up breaking away from him. That it is why I disappeared for a long time. It's because I thought he was looking for me." Shaba remembered that night in her mind, and the tears began to flood her cheeks again. "Yep, girl, he killed my sister, and it's all my fault. I shoulda never messed with him behind her back, but I just had to have everything she did. It's my fault she's gone. My fault he did what he did to her, and I'll never be able to forgive myself."

Yasmin hugged her. "Don't you do that girl. Don't you blame something like this on yourself. You didn't tell that man to do whatever he did to her. Kammron is just off his rocker. He's not all there, he needs help."

"But what do I do now? Do I go to the cops? Do I run away again? What should I do because I don't know how much longer I can't take being under his rule?" Shana cried, with her voice breaking up.

Yasmin brushed Shana's naturally curly hair out of her face and wiped away her tears. "Honey, I think you should do whatever your heart is telling you to do. The only thing about that is you have to make sure, you are doing the right things for both you and Junior. Girl, you already know how, Kammron is, he's a monster."

Shana trembled. "But if I go to the cops they'll be able to protect me, right?"

Yasmin nodded her head. "Essentially, but I also know the only way they'll be able to hold him is if they have evidence of the offense in question. If they don't all they can do is hold him up to seventy-two hours, then they'll be forced to let him go. You can already imagine what he's going to do then."

Shana's eyes got as big as saucers. "He's going to come for me."

Yasmin pursed her lips. "Unfortunately, that is more than likely the case." She felt so sympathetic for Shana. She like Shana wanted to get rid of Kammron as well. She felt Kammron's presence was the only thing holding them back from their ultimate happiness.

"Then what should I do? Should I just run away, and take Junior with me? I could fall off the face of the earth quite easily. Of, course, I'd need some sort of funds though. I think I got about five hundred dollars to my name, right now, and that ain't enough to get me far."

"I could help you in that area. Bonkers is always cashing me out for the hell of it. So, me helping you with a few thousand wouldn't be a problem. The only question is how much would you need, and where would you go?"

Shana shrugged her shoulders. "I don't have a clue. Maybe I could go to live with my father's family in Puerto Rico. They've always been so nice and welcoming. If I could hit them with a li'l' piece of change I'm sure they'd take me in."

"Well, there you go. Maybe you should give whichever one you are close to a ring on the phone or hit them up on Facebook. When you get all your ducks in a row then you can give me a call. I'll hit you with whatever you need, long as you keep it between me and you. Sound like a plan?"

Shana smiled and wiped her tears away. "So, you're saying that that is my best move?"

Yasmin shook her head in disagreement. ''Honey, I'm not saying anything. It sounds like that's what you're saying. But no matter what you decide I'm going to support you one hundred percent."

Shana came to her knees and wrapped her arms around Yasmin's neck hugging her in appreciation. "Thank you, my sister. You have no idea how thankful I truly am for you."

Yasmin rubbed her back. "Don't mention it. You focus on getting yourself together and breaking free of this monster."

"I will girl, I swear on everything I am as a woman I am." She hugged her tighter as a smile of relief spread across her face.

****

Bonner's eyes threatened to close for the eighth time. He yawned and kept his arm around Yazzy's neck. Then covered his mouth with the other one and looked over to see Kammron texting away on his phone, while the movie roared on loudly in front of them. "Yo', Son, what you over there doing?"

Kammron continued to text Jimmy. "Yo', you remember that fool Pay-Pay that Jimmy used to be real cool with back when we were li'l shorties?"

Bonkers nodded in remembrance. "Yeah, Son supposed to come up out there in Queens. He got plenty of traps jumping. Took over six Projects, and bought four restaurants, and the whole nine. Son, a major nigga now. But why, what's really good wit' Pay-Pay?"

Kammron smiled evilly. "I don't know the whole foe one-one, but it seems, Flocka flew Jimmy out to Dubai so he could handle Pay-Pay. Jimmy saying without saying, that if he do, he'll be able to open up the market in Queens as well, from the hood and slums, all the way back to Rego Park. That's a stretch, right there, son."

"But he can't do that. He and Pay-Pay practically grew up together. That a be like me snuffing you, Kid, that ain't never happening no matter the circumstances," Bonkers assured Kammron.

Yazzy put her finger to her mouth and shushed them. Her thick eyebrows were furrowed. "Please, Daddy, the movie is just getting good."

Bonkers laughed. "I'm sorry, Baby girl."

Kammron came over and kissed her on the cheek. Yo', I'm finna be out. I'ma finish hollering at Jimmy and see what it do wit' you tomorrow. Love fool." They shook up, and Kammron left the house, still texting away on his phone.

****

Jimmy stood in front of Pay-Pay with the ice pick in his right hand. Pay-Pay's mouth was dust taped, along with his eyes. Jimmy pulled the tape off his face, and eyes and stood back. He felt a sense of pity for his childhood friend.

Pay-Pay saw Jimmy and felt a sense of relief. "Jimmy, what the fuck is going on man? Tell these Jamaican mutha-fuckas I'm good bidness. That I'll help them get even richer than they could ever believe.

Flocka stepped forward with his colorful Mohawk. He had an Eagle's feather sticking in the back of it. Around his neck was three million dollars, worth of jewelry. He crouched down in front of Pay-Pay and grabbed a hold of his chin. "What was your relationship like with, Stunna?"

Pay-Pay frowned. "Your brother?"

"Yeah, my brother," Flocka responded, looking up at Jimmy.

"I was loyal to, Stunna. I kept shit one hunnit with him at all times. I'm the reason you Dellas broke into Queens," Pay-Pay assured him.

Flocka mugged him and pulled out his cellphone. He hit the button and played the recording. Pay-Pay's voice came on the phone immediately. *"Yo', trust me, Stunna, when Son come up here in a few days I'ma knock his Mohawk off, and mail it back to Jamaica to you. You'll never have to worry about, Flocka taking the throne ahead of you. Leave that to Queens."* Flocka cut the recording.

Pay-Pay struggled against his binds. "Aw shit, come on man. Why you bringing up that retro shit? That recording gotta be at least six months old." Pay-Pay looked to Jimmy. "Come on, Jimmy. Call off ya dog man, for old time's sake."

Flocka stood up. "Had I come to Queen's to conduct business with your team when I was supposed to your borough was going to see to my demise. Lucky for us there are disloyal women that sleep under you Pay-Pay. Pillow talk has been the death of a lot of good men, and even a few scum bags like yourself." Flocka snapped his fingers and held his hand up.

Felicia, Pay-Pay's wife, and a native to Jamaica stepped into the dungeon and stood beside Flocka. She handed him a briefcase. "Enclosed are all of the information to his properties, and businesses throughout Queens. The codes to his safes, offshore accounts, everything. After his death, I will be in sole power of all of them." She eyed Pay-Pay sinisterly.

Pay-Pay felt his heart drop into his stomach. "Felicia, I gave you the world. I gave you everything. How could you?" He screamed as his dark-skinned face turned reddish blue.

Flocka took the briefcase and handed it to Jimmy. "Ice this chump, and what's his is yours." He grabbed Felicia roughly and snapped her neck with a move he'd learned in the U.S. military. She fell to the floor, with her eyes wide open. Both Pay-Pay and Jimmy looked on in amazement. "Disloyal women are a cancer to a Kingpin. She comes from a family of them," Flocka chimed calmly. "Jimmy, get rid of him. You now will have the power over two boroughs. We're coming for Brooklyn next."

Jimmy stepped in front of Pay-Pay. He looked him straight in the eyes. "Yo', it's all part of the game, homie, don't take this shit personally."

Pay-Pay swallowed. "Just let me say goodbye to my daughter man. Let me say goodbye to, Leanna, that's all I ask," Pay-Pay said, swallowing a lump in his throat.

Jimmy looked over to Flocka. "What you think, Kid?"

Flocka walked over to Pay-Pay and took the cellphone out of his back pocket. He scrolled down Pay-Pay's call log until he came up on Leanna's number. He punched it in and allowed it to ring. "You got sixty seconds, you better make it good."

A moment later, Leanna came on to the phone. "Hey, Daddy, why are you calling instead of texting me?" The seventeen-year-old asked, pulling up to a stop sign in her Benz truck.

Pay-Pay felt sick to his stomach. He missed his little girl already. "Baby, Daddy just calling to say goodbye. I just wanted you to know I love you, and you are my world. Be strong for me, and I'll be looking down on from the sky."

Leanna swallowed. "Wait what? Dad, what are you talking about? You're scaring me."

"I gotta go, baby. Please be strong," Pay-Pay reiterated once again.

Leanna was crying tears of sorrow. She didn't know what to do. "Daddy, I don't know what's going on, but I love you."

"I love you with all of my heart and soul. Oh, and Jimmy killed me. Your Godfather, Jimmy did this to me! Him and Flocka the Jamaican. Jimmy is a muthafu—"

Jimmy rushed him and slammed the ice pick into his jugular over and over ten times, then stood back. Pay-Pay hunched over bleeding from the neck with his eyes wide open lifeless.

Leanna held the phone to her ear crying her heart out. "Jimmy, why-why, God Daddy?"

Flocka ended the call and looked down at Pay-Pay in disgust. Y'all clean up that mess. Jimmy, you come with me. We have a bunch of things to talk about that are going to make us both rich men."

Jimmy looked down on Pay-Pay semi-sympathetic. For as long as he'd known the man, he'd never crossed him, nor caused him any harm. The game was cutthroat though, and in order to survive inside of it, he had to move and groove as necessary. "Yeah, let's get up out of here."

T.J. Edwards

Chapter 17

It was nine at night, and Yasmin had just hung up the phone with Bonkers letting him know she was headed inside the salon to pick up her laptop. She'd told him she had a few numbers to crunch and thought it would be smart to knock the work out before she made it back home seeing as their salon was only ten blocks away from the house.

She took her keys out of her purse, and placed one inside of the lock, and opened the front door. She let herself in and closed it back locking it. The new shop had only been opened for two weeks. She had yet to get an ADT system in it like the others had. She was thinking of using a bundled package to get a lower rate. Luckily the neighborhood wasn't as bad as the rest of Harlem.

She looked around the front of the shop and saw that everything looked in place. The floor needed to be dust mopped, but it still smelled rather fresh inside of it. She set her purse on the top of a soda machine, tabbed the dust mop, and spent the next ten minutes straightening up the front of the establishment, before making her way to her office in the back of the store. She turned the lock and pushed the door in with all of Shana's drama heavy on her mind. She felt sorry for the girl, she couldn't imagine what she was going through. But she knew it had to be the worse feeling in all the world to be trapped inside of a loveless relationship with the man that was responsible for taking the life of a beloved one. She shook her head and pushed her office door all of the way open, then flipped the light switch.

"Holy shit?" She nearly jumped out of her skin at the sight on Kammron sitting behind her desk. He had two Glocks out, laying gingerly on the desktop.

Kammron mugged her and picked up one of the guns. "Close that door, Yasmin, and bring yo nosey ass in here," he ordered.

Yasmin looked over her shoulder. She thought about running. She knew Kammron would probably catch up to her if she tried to flee him, but what was her alternative? She could wind up like Shelly. *'Then what, where would that leave, Yazzy? What about, Bonkers?'* Both thoughts spooked her.

"Close the damn door, Yasmin! I'm not gon' tell you again!" He cocked the hammer and aimed at her.

Yasmin held her hands up. "Okay, Kammron, Okay. Look, just calm down." She slowly pulled the door close. "Now what?"

Kammron motioned for her to get from in front of the door. She complied. He got up, and locked it, then moved the copy machine in front of it. The office was a nice size, equipped with a desk, file cabinet, copy machine, and mini refrigerator. Even with those appliances, there was a lot of space left. Kammron curled his top lip and looked over at her. "You got a habit for poking your nose in places it don't belong."

Yasmin looked for another escape route. The only one left was the window, and now that she thought about it wasn't even an option because of the bars that were adorned on the front of it. "Kammron, I swear to, God I don't know what you're talking about. I just came to get my laptop, then Bonkers said he wanted me to come right back home or he was coming to find me."

Kammron smacked his lips. "That's bullshit, I just got off the phone with the homie. He falling off to sleep with, Yazzy in his arms. Say he got a splitting migraine."

Yasmin felt like she was ready to panic. "What do you want from me, Kammron? Just let me get my computer so I can be up out of here."

Kammron grunted. "Bitch, you shoulda known I don't trust, Shana. I got my house wired with all kinds of Siri. I heard you hoes talking about, Shelly. Heard your advice, and what you're supposedly gon' do for her." She shook his head and looked into her brown eyes. "What the fuck is wrong with you?"

Now that Yasmin knew what he knew she became afraid for her life. Her eyes were bucked wide open. "Say look Kammron, that was me just trying to be a friend. You see I steered her away from the cops. If she's willing to run away from you that's on her. I was gon' give her a little pocket change and that's it."

Kammron rubbed his chin. "Yeah, but it ain't just about her. You been putting that drag in my man's ear, too. I heard you and him talking a li'l while back, and you was saying shit like you thought it would be in his best interest to leave me behind. Yo', you got a serious problem, Shorty." He mugged her and walked in her direction.

Yasmin looked both ways and finally decided to run behind the desk. She thought about picking up the other Glock Kammron had left on the table and decided against it. For one she didn't know how to shoot it, and for two even if she knew how she didn't think she had enough nerve to do so. "Kammron, look, I'm sorry for sticking my nose where it didn't belong. From now, on I'll keep my thoughts and comments to myself. I promise you that."

Kammron looked her over and felt an intense anger wash over him. Anger coupled with lust, and irritation. He snatched the other weapon off the desk and put it into the small of his back. Grab the edge of the desk and scooted it all the way against the wall. "Yo', stop playin' wit' me shorty, and bring yo ass here."

Yasmin backed to the window. Her heart beat rampant in her chest. "Kammron, why can't you just leave me alone, and forgive me for my trespasses?"

Kammron stepped forward and put his first piece away. "Yasmin, bring yo ass over here. I'm not gon' tell you again."

Yasmin was fearful, her anxiety shot through the roof. She lowered her head, and slowly made her way over to him looking into his eyes. "What's good, Kammron?"

The closer she got to him, the more excited Kammron became. When she was standing two feet from him, he grabbed her and wrapped his arms around the small of her back. He rested his cheek against hers, inhaling the scent of her Prada perfume. His hands held her small waist and slowly traveled down to her backside. The globes poked out from her lower back. The material of the dress made it feel like she had nothing on before him. He could feel the heat of her skin, and it drove him crazy.

"Damn, it seems like yo' li'l ass getting thicker and thicker every time I see you. As much as you get on my nerves, I can't deny how crazy you drive me." He cuffed her juicy ass, and squeezed the flesh, rubbed his right hand under her cleft, and brushed his fingers over her pussy mound from the back.

Yasmin shook in his embrace. She pushed him back with mild force. "Get off me, Kammron. You already know we ain't finna get down like this. I love, Bonkers."

This only made Kammron squeeze her ass harder. He rubbed all over it and nuzzled her neck. Then licked up and down it, before sucking on it loudly. "I don't give no fuck about none of that. I ain't telling you to stop loving my man's. But you gon' develop something in your heart for me, too." He pulled up the skirt and rubbed all over her naked cheeks.

A thin strip of a thong shielded her privates. Kammron traced his finger up and down the crotch band. He felt her loose kitty lip, and the feeling drove him mad. He smushed her sex lip together in his fingers.

Yasmin moaned and tried to break free of his hold. "Stop, Kammron, please, just let me grab my laptop and go."

Kammron picked her up, and sat her on the desk, after moving everything out of the way. He sat in her office chair and rolled it in front of her. Then cocked her legs wide open and sniffed her slit. The fragrance was perfume and a hint of sweat. It gave him chills. He tightened his grip on her thighs, and pulled the crotch band to the side, peeling her dark brown lips apart, and licking up and down her crease.

Yasmin shuddered, she took a hold of his forehead and tried to push him away. Images of Bonkers danced before her eyes. She couldn't cheat on him. Not with his right-hand mans. Not with anybody. She loved him, he was her every-thing. The first man to love her in the fashion he did. She felt Kammron twirl his tongue around her clitoris. She hated her-self for moaning out loud, and involuntarily humping into his face. His big hands held her ass cheeks. He'd pushed her skirt up to her stomach and was feasting on her lowers as if he were addicted to her taste.

Kammron lifted his head. His face was greasy and drip-ping from her juices. "Dis pussy taste so good, Yasmin. Damn, you taste so fuckin' good, Shorty. I knew you would!" He went back to slurping and licking like a savage.

She jumped on the desk, whimpered, and tried to get him off her. His tongue stretched inside of her opening. It shot in and out of her, came out, and ran more circles around her vagina's nipple. She threw her head back, felt him nibbling on her down there, and the feeling became too much. The un-wanted orgasm quaked through her body and rocked her. She

T.J. Edwards

screamed and began shaking like crazy, her kitty leaked profusely.

Kammron was nasty, he licked it up and swallowed her
essence. His fingers played over the plump lips. He held them
together and kissed all over them. He could feel her shaking,
jerking. Aftershocks attacked her body. He sat back in the
chair, and pulled her on to his lap, after pulling his pants down.
His dick stood up in the air like a baseball bat.

Yasmin landed in his lap. She felt weak, she thought about
fighting him, but she found herself still highly upset for cumming so hard. She hated him as well. When she felt his head
penetrating her hole, fighting through her tunnel, a tear
dropped from her left eye. He gripped her ass and forced her
down. She consumed his entire length. Her eyes rolled into the
back of her head. She felt as guilty as sin.

Kammron felt his dick travel deep, her heat engulfed him.
She was so wet it was dripping out of her and into his lap. Her
hot breath breathed ruggedly into his face. "A'ight Ma, on my
word, I ain't gon' say shit. On my, moms in heaven, I ain't
gon' say a muthafuckin thing." He squeezed her fat ass. "Ride
me, Yasmin, ride this dick." He forced her forward.

"Uh!" she moaned with her eyes closed. Kammron's piece
was so wide, and just as long as Bonkers, the only difference
was Kammron's curved slightly. "No, Kammron!"

He pushed her away a few inches and pulled her back to
him hard. Her insides were soft, tight, and hot. He groaned and
sucked her neck. "Give me this pussy, Yasmin. His hands
traveled under her one-piece skirt and pinched her nipples.

She yelped and bucked forward. "Stop, please!"

Kammron saw that every time he pinched her nipples it
caused her to buck forward hard, so he continued to pinch the
hard nubs that stood up a half of inch. He could tell she was

heavily aroused. "Ride me, Yasmin, or I'ma pull 'em off." He pinched them harder.

Yasmin yelped and took a hold of his shoulders. She bucked forward and cocked her ass back only to move forward again. She felt Kammron filling her up, she felt so guilty.

Kammron took a hold of that ass and fucked into her. That pussy sucked at him. Every time she slammed forward, he met her with a thrust of his own. In a matter of seconds, they'd built up a steady lustful rhythm, and were moaning, and groaning. Fifteen minutes passed, and Kammron pulled her down and sucked on her neck again. He held her ass while she crashed her middle into him faster and faster.

"Shit, Yasmin, that's what I'm talking about. Uh-uh-uh, fuck dis what, uh-u-uh, I'm talking about." He bit into her neck, and came hard, splashing her walls.

Yasmin felt his hot jets spraying her, she hopped up and down. Threw her head back, and screamed, before cumming just as hard. Her breasts danced on her chest. The nipples poking toward the ceiling of the office.

Kammron stood them up, and bent her over the desk, he entered her from behind. Took hold of her hips, and long stroked her at full speed while her ass crashed into his lap jiggling like crazy. "Yasmin, uh-uh, Yasmin—fuck ma!"

Yasmin slammed back into him harder and harder. She used the edge of the desk for leverage. She could feel him in the lower portion of her stomach. His pipe felt hard as steel, and warm as a flaming sword. When he reached under her stomach and pinched her clit, she came again hard, moaning at the top of her lungs. Her knees went weak. Kammron slapped her on the ass hard and kept on piping her while holding her up.

"Kammron—Kammron, please! Uhhh-uhhh, you killing me! He gon' know, he gon' know—awwww shit!" She threw her head back and screamed as another orgasm rocked her system. She dropped to her knees.

Kammron dropped down with her and folded her up. Then he threw her legs on his shoulders and went back to work piping her fast and hard. She closed her eyes and kept her mouth wide open. Her titties jiggled up and down. Kammron hit her as hard as he could for twenty more minutes, then came hard and deep within the recesses of her womb, triggering another orgasm from her.

Chapter 18

A week later Jimmy summoned both Kammron and Bonkers to his new place in Queens, right inside Rego Park. When the men arrived, as usual, Jimmy had the dining room table loaded with food. He stood in front of it with a big smile on his face. "Welcome fellas, I already know y'all hungry. So, go wash your hands, come back, and let's fellowship. I got some stuff to put on your brains."

Kammron gazed over the table and felt his stomach growling. "Yo', this shit right on time here, Jimmy. Word up, even though I hate Queens. I gotta love this platter of food you got set before us." He gave the man half of hug and headed to the bathroom.

Bonkers looked sick, he was dealing with family issues. Ever since the day Kammron and Yasmin had done their thing she'd been incredibly distance from him, and it was eating him up on the inside. He wanted to confide in Kammron but figured the subject matter was too soft to discuss with his boys. So, instead, he suffered in silence as most killas dealing with severe depression were forced to do. He gave Jimmy a half a hug and headed in the direction of the bathroom.

As he got halfway down the hall Jimmy called out to him, "Yo', Kid, what's the deal, you good?" he asked, concerned for his little brother.

Bonkers nodded. "Yeah, just dealing with a headache," he lied. "You know how the game go."

Jimmy smiled weakly. He could tell Bonkers wasn't being honest with him. 'Yeah, A'ight, Kid, fuck wit' me in a minute though."

Bonkers hunched his shoulders and made it to Jimmy's bathroom where Kammron was washing his hands. He grabbed a bar of soap and proceeded to do the same.

Kammron began drying his hands. "Yo', what's really good wit' you, Kid? It seems like something is a little off with you." He looked Bonkers over closely.

Bonkers shrugged his shoulders. "I'm just dealing with some personal issues, I'll be alright. Shorty driving me crazy and have been for the last week, that's all."

Kammron laughed. "Yo', that's that family life, Dunn. I still can't see how you can be under the same woman every day all day. Yo', that takes some kind of nigga to be able to do that, word to the Pimps before me man."

Bonkers fake laughed. "Yasmin, a good girl, bruh. She means well, she one hunnit. But no matter what I gotta keep our family structure strong for, Yazzy. Every couple go through those rough times, we'll be alright."

Kammron's A.D.D. kicked in. He began imagining how Yasmin's pussy looked when he spread the brown lips all the way open. Her kitty's insides were strawberry colored. Her fit was snug, and her scent made him feel some type of way.

Bonkers nudged him. "You heard what I said?"

Kammron nodded, even though he hadn't. "Yo', y'all gon be alright. I get a good feeling from, Shorty, she straight in my eyes." Kammron handed him the towel and left out of me the bathroom with Bonkers standing there perplexed.

For as long as Yasmin had been back in the picture he had never once heard Kammron say anything about liking her. He washed his hands and followed him into the other room where they were to sit down and have a feast alongside Jimmy.

****

Kammron ripped the meat from the bone with his teeth, and chewed the Turkey loudly, holding the huge drumstick in his hand. "So, you mean to tell me, you're trying to move

156

inside of Queens now? Bruh, we don't know nothing about Queens, at least I don't. Why the fuck would we be moving into that territory when we ain't even got Harlem all the way under control?"

Kammron forked some of the dressing into his mouth, along with a bit of cranberry sauce. He started chewing it all together with his eyes closed, and a slight smile on his face.

Bonkers picked at his fool. He really didn't have an appetite. He was too busy fixating on the beef between him and Yasmin, even though he didn't know what they were beefing for. He could simply feel it deep within his soul.

Jimmy wiped his mouth with a Burberry handkerchief. "It's pure and simple." He took a sip of the red wine and swished it around his mouth. "You see when it comes to the game Harlem, and Harlem taking it over, in order for Harlem to do so, it means Harlem has to conquer as many of the other boroughs as it can. Queen's is a start, Flocka is thinking Brooklyn next. Although that task is going to be a little harder than the other boroughs because of the Vega family. Showbiz is currently waiting for his seat on the throne, and that will prove problematic for us Ponces'. He hates our entire bloodline no matter how much he tries to make it seem he doesn't.

"It's been that way ever since I whooped his ass in front of our class, after our field trip when we went to Fidel Elementary in the fifth grade. Ever since then we have been sworn, enemies. If Vito passes the throne down to him there is going to be a major war here in New York, and back home in Cuba. The Ponces' and the Vegas' has been walking on eggshells around one another for over a hundred years. Our sugar cane fields separated each other's by only about fifty acres. My father Ruiz, and Vito Vega were old running buddies and worked under Fidel before he caked into power. They have history and have done a lot of dirt together. They respect one another. It's only the children that do not respect each other."

Kammron sprinkled sugar over his rice and added butter. He was entranced by the story Jimmy was telling him regarding the Ponce's family history. It was fascinating and sucked because he had no clue where his family's history started.

"Yo', but what about the other son, Tristan. I heard he's also in a position to take over Vito's seat after he steps down because of his illness. Wouldn't it be smart for us to befriend him instead of waging war with the Vegas?" Bonkers asked.

Jimmy nodded. "Of course, but that is easier said than done. Tristan follows behind Showbiz, right now. He's like his hero, so until further notice we have to look at him as just as much of a threat as Showbiz."

Kammron unbuttoned the top button of his Fendi pants and sat back in the chair. His stomach was poked out because he was so full. He scratched his tummy. "A'ight Kid, get back to the whole Queens thing. Who do we have to go through in order to make Queens become an official territory of Harlem? Connect the boroughs into one so to speak?"

Jimmy stood up and drank directly from the bottle of Merlot. His Versace robe hung open enough to show off his rockhard abs, and muscular chest. He was tatted from collarbone to waist. The words 'Da Capo' in bold was across his chest. "Queens is no longer a problem. Pay-Pay was in charge, and let's just say, Pay-Pay is no longer a factor."

Bonkers gave him a strange look. "What you saying, Jimmy? You tryna say, Kid, been snuffed a something?"

Jimmy felt a twinge of remorse for Pay-Pay. "Yo', it's real out here in the field, Dunn. It's no holds barred. Ma'fuckas out here dying every day. It's kill or be killed. Rise and fall, put up or shut up."

"Yo', you doing plenty talking, Kid. Is the nigga dead or alive? Fuck!" Kammron asked rolling his eyes. He hated long drawn out explanations.

Jimmy mugged him. "He's deceased, per Flocka's orders."

Bonkers was taken aback. "Yo', that nigga, Pay-Pay was your homie man. I'm taking it like you wasted him, damn. It seems like this dude, Flocka is really the one running Harlem and taking over Queens. And you're his flunky. What happens when he gives you the order to knock off one of us? What will you do then?" Bonkers was in disbelief. No matter what the game called for he knew he could never hurt either Kammron or Jimmy. It just wasn't in his nature to do so.

Jimmy was starting to get angry. He felt Bonkers had a valid point about Pay-Pay and that irritated him. Secondly, the irritation came from the realization that he may have actually been Flocka's flunky, and he didn't like playing second fiddle to any man. He tilted his head to the ceiling and took a deep breath. "Yo', I swear I wish you li'l' niggas could be at the head for a second, and y'all could see how difficult all this shit is to navigate. Bruh, stuff getting thrown at me from every angle all day long, and it's my job to navigate this ship accordingly."

"Fuck that got to do wit' you answering the homie question, Jimmy?" Kammron interrupted him. "Nigga, if he gave you the order to wet one of us would you do it or not?"

"Hell nall, damn, Kammron. You should already know that shit. Do you know how wild you li'l niggas are? Before y'all came under me y'all were robbing and doing all kinds of dumb shit. Do you know how many times you muthafuckas names have come up on the short list for execution, huh?"

Kammron cheesed. 'That's cuz we be given the Apple the bidness. These niggas be praying for our demise. The God trigger happy. I'm getting good wit' a Kitana, too." He closed his eyes and drank from his Champagne.

Jimmy shook his head and sighed. "Anyway, we're family. Bonkers you are my blood brother, and Kammron in my eyes you are as well. I would never desert or bring harm to either of you no matter what happened in this life. I love both of you li'l niggas."

"Ah, ah, ah." Kammron held up a chastising finger. "Miss us with that li'l nigga crap, Kid. You said you was done calling us that. We young bosses, Harlem greats." Kammron held his bottle of Moët in the air and poured it from that distance. The liquid fell into his mouth, and some splashed off his teeth wetting his cheeks.

Bonkers snickered. "Yo', Jimmy, it's good, Kid. I love you, too! I know you been under the barrel because of me and Killa over the years. We appreciate you for holding us down more than you'll ever know. A'ight but let us know what the move is wit' this whole Queens thing. What are you seeing?

As soon as Bonkers finished his sentence the doorbell to Jimmy's door rang. Jimmy frowned and pulled two .44 Desert Eagles out of his robe from their holsters and made his way toward the front of the house. He peeked out of the curtain and saw that the entire curb in front of his house was filled with parked red Benzs, and Jaguars. There was even one parked in his driveway. On his porch step stood Tristan Vega. Behind him were two Brooklyn Shooters with mugs on their faces. Jimmy jumped back. His heart beating fast, and hard.

From a distance, Kammron saw the look on his face and already sensed trouble. He pulled out both of his Glocks and ran toward the back of the house. He opened the backdoor, and rushed down the steps headed for the backyard, then to the gangway that led to the front of the house. He figured if they were about to be under attack than he would take as many with him as he possibly could.

Bonkers grabbed the M-90 out of the guest room and slammed a hundred round magazine inside of it. He ran beside Jimmy. "What it do fool?"

Jimmy was already texting for his security to get on point. One group text and he had his Hittas traveling at full speed toward the destination. Twenty of them had already been in route. He peeked back out of the window again. Now there were five shooters that pulled up on red Ducattis. They wore all black, with ski masks over their faces. This made Jimmy nervous. His forehead began to perspire. He closed the curtain back and paced back and forth.

"Yo', it seems like we talked these niggas up man. That's that dude Tristan, right there."

Bonkers cocked the M-90. "Yo', fuck we waiting on? If we give them the jump, they gon' get the better of us. I ain't on that shit, I'm finna let these niggas have it." Bonkers pressed his back to the wall and peeked out of the curtain. He saw more of the Vega family troops pulling up and became apprehensive of their outcome. Then it hit him that Kammron was missing. "Fuck is, Kammron?"

Jimmy's brain was racing a million miles an hour. He felt sick. He'd just began to taste what the high life felt like. He wasn't ready to die already. He needed to think of a way to get out of the position he found himself in.

Tristan stepped forward and knocked on the door three times real hard. "Yo', Jimmy, I come in peace, Kid. Ain't nobody finna buck these gats, this is just how I roll. Open up the door, or I'ma be forced to turn this bitch out," he threatened.

Bonkers bit into his lower lip. "Fuck is we finna do? Is it on or not?" He tapped his trigger and ignited the blue beam on top of the fully automatic weapon.

Kammron jogged into the front room. "Yo', dem niggas all up and down the alley, Kid. They all on the side of the gangway heavily armed. Ain't no way out of this shit. I guess we finna go out in a blaze of glory." He sat on the couch and poured some of the North Korean on the table, before taking two lines to the head hard.

Bonkers sat beside him and cleared two as well. "Yo', let's ice these punks, bruh. My word, I love you to the end, Dunn. That's on my moms." He hugged him and felt a twinge of remorse for Yazzy. He missed his baby girl. He wished he could see her one more time, but the game was what the game was. You were here today and gone tomorrow. That is the way the cookie crumbled.

Kammron hopped up. "Let's handle this bidness. It's Harlem son, word to Jehovah!" He rushed toward the front of the house ready to unleash a barrage of bullets through the window.

Bonkers jumped up to cover him, after crossing himself with the crucifix. "Let's get it!" He placed the beam on Tristan's head from the window and closed one eye. "Fuck nigga, it's a wrap."

Chapter 19

"Wait—just wait!" Jimmy hollered, grabbing Bonkers wrist. "Just wait, let me squash this beef, Kid. At the very least let me hear Son out to see what he talking about."

Bonkers frowned and stood back. He rested the M-90 against his shoulder. "Yo', that's suicide. Them niggas deep out there. They don't look like they ready to talk."

"Yeah, Dunn, them Vega boys out there deep. It's either we get to clapping at their ass, or they finna give us a round of applause. I ain't trying to be on nobodies receiving end," Kammron let it be known.

Jimmy held up his hand. "If they was on that gunplay they woulda came spraying instead of knocking on the door, think about it." Jimmy pulled the curtain back that covered the top of the door's window. He opened it just a crack. "Yo', what's good, Tristan? What brings you all the way here from Red Hook?"

Tristan smiled and dusted off his black fatigues. "I come in the name of peace and understanding. I think it will be in your best interest to have a sit down with me before things take a turn for the worse. You'll find out that me and my brother have two different styles of negotiation. Out of respect for your father, Ruiz, and my father, I thought I should come and holler at you while he is still back in Havana trying to get the green light to blow you, and your establishment off the map. So, if you'll invite me in, we can sit down as business-men and come to an agreement.

Kammron shook his head and mouthed the words. "Fuck that nigga, blast his ass."

Jimmy waved him off and stuck his head out of the door. "Yo', tell your hittas to ease up. I'll allow you to bring two of your security guards inside, but that's it. You and I can come to the table and get an understanding."

Tristan shook his head. "No can do, meet me here at this address tomorrow, and we'll have a power lunch." He handed him a card for a restaurant in Brooklyn. "We'll sit down and get an understanding to see if we can fix this power struggle for New York. You have my word, not a hair will be touched on your head. I swear on my mother." He placed his right hand over his heart.

Jimmy looked the address over. "Yo', this in Buck Town. I got mad enemies out that way, Kid. We gon' have to pick another spot, but the time is good."

Tristan bowed in submission. "Tell you what, you pick the location, and I'll be there at ten o'clock sharp. Just hit my phone with the location. Until then, keep ya head up." He turned to his men, and signaled for them to load up, and move out. Jimmy looked on with fascination and jealousy. As soon as Tristan's people had vacated the premises for thirty seconds Jimmy's pulled up, six jeeps deep ready for war. They hopped out with fully automatics and extended clips.

Jimmy met them on the street, still feeling jealous by the discipline he'd saw in Tristan's troops. "Yo', we gotta tighten up this shit way more than what it is. Y'all making me look like a fuckin' sucka?" he snapped. He looked down the street, as Tristan's people's brake lights were still visible to him.

Kammron walked over to Bonkers and leaned into his ear. "Yo', Kid, I know we following behind your brother and shit, but I think it's time we established ourselves. Jimmy looked mad spooked a few minutes ago. He didn't want that gunplay, Bonkers. I think that money making him soft as baby shit."

Bonkers had peeped the same thing. "You might be right, Kammron. I didn't like what I saw either. We were the only two ready to go to war with all them niggas. You are only as strong as your head, and right now our head weak as a wimp."

"Say, fuck is you gon' do, Jimmy? You gon' actually go and meet with that fool or what?" Kammron hollered.

Jimmy walked up the steps, and past them, after sending his Hittas away. "That's exactly what I'ma do." He was defeated. Tristan had shown him he had a long way to go before he considered himself a Don, or even a Capo.

****

That night when Bonkers got home he found Yasmin sitting up in the living room smoking a cigarillo, which was extremely uncharacteristic of her. She was listening to Harlem's own Keith Sweat. She looked him over from the corner of her eyes and shook her head.

Bonkers gazed down the hallway toward their bedroom. He placed both of his Glocks on the couch and sat down across from Yasmin. He looked the table over and saw there was a zip of Loud. This made him angry. "Yo, what are you doing in here? And where did you get this bud from?"

Yasmin finished rolling her rello and ran a lighter up and down the length of it. After drying it, she lit the tip, and puffed on it two times, inhaling hard. She closed her eyes and blew the smoke to the ceiling. "Where you been at, Bonkers? Are you out sleeping around on me?"

Bonkers mugged her. "What?"

She took another pull and inhaled it hard. Already her high discovered her. "You heard what I asked you, Bonkers. What, this family ain't worth holding together no more?" She set the cigarillo in the ashtray and stared at him.

Bonkers curled his upper lip. "Shorty, what the fuck is you in here on, huh? You been waiting ya ass up all night just so when I walked in, we could get in this punk ass argument, that it?"

Yasmin pursed her lips, she picked the cigarillo back up and shook her head. "You know something, Bonkers. You men are all alike. All y'all do is cheat, play mind games, and make shit incredibly difficult for a woman. I'm so tired of your conniving ways that I don't know what to do. This shit ain't for me no more, though. I tried, I swear I really really did." She stood up, still puffing on the ganja.

Bonkers sat there for a moment perplexed. The first person he thought about was Yazzy, and how their separation would affect her. He swallowed his spit, sick at the thought of his family separating. Then he grew angry, he hopped up and followed Yasmin into their master bedroom.

Yasmin sat on the bed and stubbed the cigarillo out. She was lifted, high as a kite. She felt free, and with an insane amount of courage. "Don't bring ya ass in here giving me some lecture, Bonkers. I ain't got time for that shit," she warned him.

Bonkers came inside the room and closed the door. He walked over to her and grabbed her by the hair, she yelped. He pulled her up and placed her against the wall. "Yasmin, if you don't tell me what the fuck yo problem is on, my daughter I'm finna surf yo ass, right here, and right now. I'm tired of playin' these games wit' you. What the fuck if the problem?"

Yasmin closed her eyes, breathing hard. She opened them slowly and peered into his. "I'm tired, Bonkers, I don't know if I can do this shit no more. I think I need a change of pace. Now let me go."

Bonkers clenched his jaw, he mugged her with increasing anger. "And what the fuck brought this on?"

"Didn't nothing bring it on. I'm just tired all around the board. I'm tired of waiting up for you every night worrying if you coming home. I'm tired of sitting back being this good wife without the ring. The good wife knowing you're out there dogging me. I'm too young to be playin' this role. It's as simple as that. Now can you please get out of my face."

Bonkers looked into her eyes for fifteen seconds longer and released her. He turned his back to her. He couldn't believe none of the things she was saying. He lowered his head. "Yo', why the fuck is you coming at me with this drag, Shorty? A mafucka been one hunnit to you ever since we been staying under the same roof. Damn, you had a nigga seeing forever and all of that. Now all of a sudden you just want us to up and part. What happened to giving our daughter the two-parent household that we never had? Whatever happened to us doing right by her?"

Yasmin's eyes were misty. "I guess, I'm just not cut out for this. I really tried, Bonkers. You gotta believe me when I tell you I really tried." She sat on the bed and covered her face. All of the guilt from what she'd done with Kammron had fully started to take over her. She was tired of walking around their house not being able to look him in the eye without feeling like a whore, or less than a woman. It had never been in her to cheat. Now that she had she felt like dirt like he deserved somebody better than her.

Bonkers felt weak, and a twinge of emotion. "Yo', I can't believe this shit is happening. Nah, fuck that." He turned to Yasmin and kneeled in front of her. "Say ma, I love you more than life. I ain't trying to lose you, or our family. You mean the world to me, and I'm willing to die for you, our child, and our relationship. You're my Eve, Yasmin. Only you, ain't no female worthy to be my Queen other than you. If you want me to make it official, yo' I'd do that with no problem. My word to Jehovah man, you're so so worth it."

167

Yasmin squeezed tears out of her eyes. She imagined Kammron hitting her hard from the back. She saw their forbidden tryst, and her not putting up a fight, and it made her sick to the stomach. She'd betrayed the one and only man in who she knew truly loved her. "No, Bonkers, we can't do this no more. I don't know what we're going to do, but to be honest you deserve a Queen much better than me." She placed her hands over her face again and broke down crying.

Bonkers choked up, he started to feel broken. His mind wouldn't work in the way he needed it too. He felt like he needed a fix. He looked up at her, then stood up. "Yo', I don't know what's going on, but I need a minute. You're making me really feel some type of way, right now. And before I put my hands on you, I'ma go in this bathroom and take a breather." He turned his back to her and walked off.

Yasmin sat on the bed and cried her eyes out. She wanted to tell him so bad what happened between her and Kammron. Wanted to tell him she was sorry. That she would never cheat on him again, that she had no choice. She wanted to beg for forgiveness. To get it all out in the open, so her conscious could be eased, but instead, she sat on the bed sobbing her eyes out.

Bonkers stepped into the bathroom, and the first thing he saw on the sink was a pregnancy test. He picked up the stick and saw that it was positive. His eyes got bucked. "You're pregnant. You mean to tell me you're pregnant, and you're trying to pull this shit?" He asked walking back into the bedroom with the stick in his hand.

Yasmin froze, uncovered her face, and stood up. She felt exposed. She'd forgotten about the positive pregnancy test. She was beating herself up for being so careless. "It's not important, Bonkers." '*Especially since I don't know whose baby it is*,' she wanted to yell at him. '*I don't know if it's yours or*

Kammron's,' she wanted to scream at the top of her lungs before she sunk deeper into depression, and pure frustration. But instead, she held her peace and held in the secret that was plaguing her soul.

Bonkers exhaled loudly and mugged her with hatred. "Yo', I don't know where this cold shit coming from? But you driving me crazy, right now, Yasmin. I'm holding a fuckin' pregnancy test in my hands and you making it seem like it's not a big fuckin' deal!" He squeezed the pregnancy stick in his hand and clenched his jaw with mounting anger.

Yasmin shrugged her shoulders. "This is just the way it is Bonkers. I'm going through something, right now. I don't know what else to tell you." She was crying again, and seconds away from telling about her betrayal. She could barely look him in the eyes, because every time she looked at him, she could tell he was disgusted by her actions.

Bonkers mugged her for a long time and sucked his teeth. "You know what? I been in these mafuckin' streets grinding and putting my life on the line for this family. I been one hunnit to you ever since we confirmed Yazzy was my daughter. I been looking at you like a wife instead of one of these bitches in the street, and this is the thanks I get. I'm holding a mafuckin' pregnancy test in my hand, and you're telling me you no longer wanna be with me?" He tossed the test at her and of ricocheted off her rib and fell to the bed? "Well, fuck you then! As much as I love you, Yasmin, I'm not gon' beg you to stay wit' me. But you not finna breakup this family. My daughter deserves both of her parents, and that's exactly what it's gon' appear that she has. That's just that."

Yasmin's face was soaked with tears now. "So, what are you saying Bonkers. What do you want me to do, I'm just lost, right now baby?"

Bonkers looked her over with disgust. "You know what, Yasmin, the way I'm feeling, right now! I really don't give a fuck what you do. But I'ma keep on doing what I gotta do for you, for our daughter, and for that child, we have on the way. I don't know what you're going through, but I still got you." He kissed her on the forehead and left out of the room fuming.

Yasmin lowered her head and broke down worse than she ever had before. "Bonkers, I'm sorry baby. I'm so so sorry, I slept with, Kammron! I cheated on you, Daddy, and I don't know if the baby is his or yours!" She fell from the bed to her knees on the carpet.

Bonkers stood in the hallway for a moment with his hands resting on the wall. He dropped his head and shook it slowly, then sighed, loaded up his guns, and left the house feeling murderous.

Chapter 20

Kammron scratched the back of his neck, with his eyes closed. He smacked his lips and took another line of the North Korean straight to the dome. "Yo', Kid shorty sound like she wilding out. How the fuck she gon' be pregnant, then talking about she wanna leave?" He asked shaking his head.

Bonkers sat across the table from him with his hand on the handle of his Glock under his shirt. It was a week after Yasmin had told him what she'd done regarding her and Kammron sleeping around behind his back. After he inquired further, she'd broke down and told him everything from beginning to end. Bonkers had been so heated, he had to stay holed up in a hotel for an entire week. Bonkers eyed Kammron from across the table? "That shit do sound real fishy don't it?"

Kammron was high as heaven, his eyelids drooped. "Yo', that's why I say the world is too big to be investing all of your time and energy into one bitch. Word is bond, I don't give a fuck if she got a baby by me or not." He pulled his nose and smacked his lips loudly.

Bonkers felt his heart turning cold, as Jimmy walked into the room smoking on a Cuban cigar. He took a swallow from his orange and pineapple juice. "Yo', we gon' have plenty of time to talk about them hoes, B. Right now, we need to have a sit-down and talk about how we finna take over Queens, while at the same time keeping Harlem in check. It's a crazy world out there, and them Vegas are only making shit crazier."

Bonkers waved Jimmy off. "Later for that bullshit, I need to holler at Kammron for a minute."

"What?" Jimmy asked, taken completely off guard.

Kammron was nodding in and out. He was so high he could hardly keep his eyes open. He tilted his head back and scratched his inner forearm again. "Kid, what you gotta holler at me about?"

"Why do you think, Yasmin, flexing on me when it comes to her pregnancy? You got something you wanna tell me?" He asked clutching the handle of his Glock even tighter.

Kammron smiled and ran his hand across his face. "Yo', why the fuck would I have anything to tell you, Dunn? You the one been running around trying to wife hoes and shit. It ain't got nothing to do wit' me." He opened his eyes and looked over at Bonkers.

Jimmy saw where this conversation was going. It was clear to him Bonkers thought Kammron had something going on with Yasmin, and he was beating around the bush and afraid to ask him. He decided to cut to the chase. Yo', Kammron, you got something going on with, Yasmin?"

Kammron snickered and pulled his nose. "I'm, Killa Kamm. The god ain't fuckin wit' no bitch, life is too short for all that being locked down shit. So, my answer is no." He closed his eyes for a second, then opened them back and looked Bonkers over.

Bonkers mugged him. "Kid, I been fuckin' wit' you ever since we been li'l project babies. I've always been one hunnit wit' you. I've always kept shit thorough, and I thought you was carrying on the same way. Nigga, I need to know what happened between you and my bitch the night of the barbecue. The same night she went to pick up her laptop. She telling me one thing, but I need to hear what's really good from you. So, why don't you keep shit one hunnit and give me your side of things."

Kammron laughed. "Nigga, you got the game fucked up. It ain't my bidness to get in y'all bidness. I don't know what, Shorty could possibly tell you about me because I don't fuck wit' her at all. I stay in my own lane. I got enough shit on my plate, then to have to be worried about what you got going on wit' yo bitch. That sucka for love shit ain't in me."

Bonkers clenched his jaw. "Nigga, I'ma ask you one time, did you force yourself on, Yasmin?" Bonkers took out the gun and set it on the table, he'd already cocked it.

Now Kammron's eyes were opened wide. He mugged the gun on the table, and slowly trailed his eyes up to those of Bonkers. "Nigga, this what this shit is coming down to?" Kammron upped two pistols, and slammed them on the table, then pointed both barrels at Bonkers. His high dwindled just a tad.

Jimmy was shocked. "What the fuck y'all in here doing? I know you two li'l niggas ain't about to fall off over no bitch?" He looked from one young man to the other one. He was shocked that things had gotten so far.

Bonkers curled his upper lip. "Nigga, did you force my bitch or not?"

Kammron ran his tongue across his teeth. "I ain't forced your bitch to do shit. Nigga, I ain't even been wit' her under that context. I don't know why she lying on me, but once again I ain't got time to be worrying about another nigga's bitch. Life is too short."

Jimmy sat at the table. "Yo,' are y'all kidding me, right now? You two are homies, nall matter fact, y'all are brothers. I know damn well y'all ain't about to fall off over no female? Especially when we just starting to get our money all the way up the way it's supposed to be."

Bonkers lowered his eyes and continued to mug Kammron. "Nigga, I love you, I'll die for you any second of the day. I care about you more than I do my own blood brother. I just need to know if you and Shorty fucked around? If y'all did and that shit was mutual then I can deal wit' that. But if y'all did, and it wasn't then we finna have some major problems. Third to that if she lying, I gotta holler at this girl, because I know she don't like you, and if she's only saying this shit to drive a wedge between us then I can't let that slide. I'ma have to handle my views accordingly. So, I'ma ask you one more time, bruh what was the real deal?

Kammron was not finna let Yasmin divide them. He'd already had it in his mind, he was going to get rid of her for the long run at his earliest convenience, but the first thing he needed to do was fuck Bonkers' head up. After he accomplished that task, he would be free to go at Yasmin in the manner he needed to.

"Yo', on all the love I have for you, Bonkers, and on my word to Kathy, I never fucked, Yasmin. And I never would have," he lied. "If I even thought she would go I woulda told you right away. You already know I ain't on that cuffing no bitch type shit, anyway. But me and her ain't even been alone before. I don't know why she kicking up this bullshit, but I'm ready to confront her in front of you. That's the only way you gon' find out who lying. Once you see that I'm keeping shit one hunnit you'll be able to make the right decision. But I'm letting you know right now that it ain't me."

Bonkers grabbed his gun from the table and stood up. "Nigga, we definitely gon' do exactly that. I'ma sit both of y'all down tonight, and we gon' get to the bottom of all of this."

Kammron kept his guns on the table and walked up to Bonkers. He held out his hand and gave him half of hug. "Yo', it ain't nothing but love, Kid. Just another obstacle we gotta climb. In the end, I'ma be that nigga holding you down as usual. What time you trying to have this sit down?"

Bonkers rubbed his chin. "Shorty, get off work at eleven tonight because she gotta go over a few things. She usually make it home about fifteen minutes after eleven. We gon' have that sit down right then. Gon' get to the bottom of all of this shit."

Kammron hugged him again. "That sounds good to me, I'll make sure I be there. "

Jimmy placed his hand on Bonkers' shoulder. "Now that y'all got this stuff figured out, for the most part, we need to focus on bigger and better things. Like getting money and staying rich. Bitches gon' come and go, but our love for one another has to be forever," Jimmy reminded them.

In the back of his mind, he was feeling some type of way about Bonkers saying he basically loved Kammron more than he did him, and they were blood. But it was a topic he would bring up at another time. At the moment he needed both men to be on their game. They had a huge task ahead of them, especially since talks with Tristan Vega had fallen through. Tristan had told Jimmy, Showbiz would stop at nothing until he'd broken Jimmy and all of Harlem down into pieces. He told Jimmy, Showbiz Vega was out for more than blood, he wanted to humiliate him, and anybody associated with him.

Tristan thought a war was bad for business, but Showbiz was dead set on wiping out Jimmy before he did anything else. Their father Chico Vega was dying swiftly, soon he would name a successor, and if it, was Showbiz that spelled lethal trouble for everything Jimmy had built. Tristan wanted Jimmy to come to some form of an understanding with Showbiz, but his hatred was just a bad, so there was no reasoning with either man. The only other option was war and murder.

"I'm taking a trip out to Jamaica so I can holler at Flocka face to face. I'll be back in a few days, then we're going into overdrive. I need y'all to have ya game faces on. Either one of y'all got a problem with that?"

Bonkers shook his head. "I need to get my house in order. Once I find out what the deal is, I can move forward, but not until that time. It's as simple as that."

Kammron smiled sadistically. He already had smoking Yasmin on his mind. His plan was to get to her job first so he could waste her before she had a chance to make it home. With her out of the picture, he and Bonkers could go back to the way things once were. The thought of Yazzy irritated him but not as much as Yasmin. He would take care of her later as well, though? He'd already convinced himself of that. "I feel the homie, and I can only imagine how much it's fuckin' wit' his mind. We gon' nip this shit in the bud tonight? Then we'll be able to go at the city of New York's throat."

Jimmy nodded. "Yeah, y'all get that shit under control so we can take over this—"

The front room window shattered, and a pepper bomb was tossed into it. Then another window shattered, and two smoke pepper bombs traveled through it as well, It was followed by a loud explosion before rapid gunfire erupted. Jimmy's house filled with dark, grey smoke and the trio found themselves under attack.

To Be Continued
Coke Kings 3
Coming Soon…

Submission Guideline

Submit the first three chapters of your completed manuscript to ldpsubmissions@gmail.com, subject line: Your book's title. The manuscript must be in a .doc file and sent as an attachment. Document should be in Times New Roman, double spaced and in size 12 font. Also, provide your synopsis and full contact information. If sending multiple submissions, they must each be in a separate email.

Have a story but no way to send it electronically? You can still submit to LDP/Ca$h Presents. Send in the first three chapters, written or typed, of your completed manuscript to:

LDP: Submissions Dept
Po Box 870494
Mesquite, Tx 75187

DO NOT send original manuscript. Must be a duplicate.

Provide your synopsis and a cover letter containing your full contact information.

Thanks for considering LDP and Ca$h Presents.

T.J. Edwards

<u>Coming Soon from Lock Down Publications/Ca$h Presents</u>

BOW DOWN TO MY GANGSTA

By **Ca$h**

TORN BETWEEN TWO

By **Coffee**

BLOOD STAINS OF A SHOTTA **III**

By **Jamaica**

STEADY MOBBIN **III**

By **Marcellus Allen**

BLOOD OF A BOSS **VI**

By **Askari**

LOYAL TO THE GAME **IV**

LIFE OF SIN **III**

By **T.J. & Jelissa**

A DOPEBOY'S PRAYER **II**

By **Eddie "Wolf" Lee**

IF LOVING YOU IS WRONG… **III**

LOVE ME EVEN WHEN IT HURTS **III**

By **Jelissa**

TRUE SAVAGE **VII**

By **Chris Green**

BLAST FOR ME **III**

DUFFLE BAG CARTEL **IV**

By **Ghost**

ADDICTIED TO THE DRAMA **III**

By **Jamila Mathis**

A HUSTLER'S DECEIT 3

KILL ZONE **II**

BAE BELONGS TO ME III

SOUL OF A MONSTER II

By **Aryanna**

THE COST OF LOYALTY **III**

By **Kweli**

SHE FELL IN LOVE WITH A REAL ONE **II**

By **Tamara Butler**

RENEGADE BOYS **III**

By **Meesha**

CORRUPTED BY A GANGSTA **IV**

By **Destiny Skai**

A GANGSTER'S SYN II

By **J-Blunt**

KING OF NEW YORK V

RISE TO POWER III

COKE KINGS III

By **T.J. Edwards**

GORILLAZ IN THE BAY III

De'Kari

THE STREETS ARE CALLING II

Duquie Wilson

KINGPIN KILLAZ IV

STREET KINGS 2

PAID IN BLOOD 2

Hood Rich

SINS OF A HUSTLA II

ASAD

TRIGGADALE II

Elijah R. Freeman

MARRIED TO A BOSS III

By Destiny Skai & Chris Green

KINGZ OF THE GAME III

Playa Ray

SLAUGHTER GANG II

By Willie Slaughter

THE HEART OF A SAVAGE II

By Jibril Williams

FUK SHYT II

By Blakk Diamond

THE DOPEMAN'S BODYGAURD II

By Tranay Adams

Available Now

RESTRAINING ORDER **I & II**

By **CA$H & Coffee**

LOVE KNOWS NO BOUNDARIES **I II & III**

By **Coffee**

RAISED AS A GOON I, II, III & IV

BRED BY THE SLUMS I, II, III

BLAST FOR ME I & II

ROTTEN TO THE CORE I II III
A BRONX TALE I, II, III
DUFFEL BAG CARTEL I II III
By **Ghost**
LAY IT DOWN **I & II**
LAST OF A DYING BREED
BLOOD STAINS OF A SHOTTA I & II
By **Jamaica**
LOYAL TO THE GAME
LOYAL TO THE GAME II
LOYAL TO THE GAME III
LIFE OF SIN I, II
By **TJ & Jelissa**
BLOODY COMMAS I & II
SKI MASK CARTEL I II & III
KING OF NEW YORK I II,III IV
RISE TO POWER I II
COKE KINGS I II
By **T.J. Edwards**
IF LOVING HIM IS WRONG…I & II
LOVE ME EVEN WHEN IT HURTS I II
By **Jelissa**
WHEN THE STREETS CLAP BACK I & II III
By **Jibril Williams**
A DISTINGUISHED THUG STOLE MY HEART I II & III
LOVE SHOULDN'T HURT I II III IV
RENEGADE BOYS I & II

By **Meesha**

A GANGSTER'S CODE I &, II III

A GANGSTER'S SYN

By J-Blunt

PUSH IT TO THE LIMIT

By **Bre' Hayes**

BLOOD OF A BOSS **I, II, III, IV, V**

By **Askari**

THE STREETS BLEED MURDER **I, II & III**

THE HEART OF A GANGSTA I II& III

By **Jerry Jackson**

CUM FOR ME

CUM FOR ME 2

CUM FOR ME 3

CUM FOR ME 4

An **LDP Erotica Collaboration**

BRIDE OF A HUSTLA **I II & II**

THE FETTI GIRLS **I, II& III**

CORRUPTED BY A GANGSTA I, II & III

By **Destiny Skai**

WHEN A GOOD GIRL GOES BAD

By **Adrienne**

THE COST OF LOYALTY

By Kweli

A GANGSTER'S REVENGE **I II III & IV**

THE BOSS MAN'S DAUGHTERS

THE BOSS MAN'S DAUGHTERS II

THE BOSSMAN'S DAUGHTERS III

THE BOSSMAN'S DAUGHTERS IV

THE BOSS MAN'S DAUGHTERS **V**

A SAVAGE LOVE **I & II**

BAE BELONGS TO ME I II

A HUSTLER'S DECEIT I, II, III

WHAT BAD BITCHES DO I, II, III

SOUL OF A MONSTER

By **Aryanna**

A KINGPIN'S AMBITON

A KINGPIN'S AMBITION **II**

I MURDER FOR THE DOUGH

By **Ambitious**

TRUE SAVAGE

TRUE SAVAGE II

TRUE SAVAGE **III**

TRUE SAVAGE **IV**

TRUE SAVAGE **V**

TRUE SAVAGE **VI**

By **Chris Green**

A DOPEBOY'S PRAYER

By **Eddie "Wolf" Lee**

THE KING CARTEL **I, II & III**

By **Frank Gresham**

THESE NIGGAS AIN'T LOYAL **I, II & III**

By **Nikki Tee**

GANGSTA SHYT **I II &III**

T.J. Edwards

By **CATO**
<u>THE ULTIMATE BETRAYAL</u>
By **Phoenix**
<u>BOSS'N UP **I , II & III**</u>
By **Royal Nicole**
<u>I LOVE YOU TO DEATH</u>
By Destiny J
<u>I RIDE FOR MY HITTA</u>
<u>I STILL RIDE FOR MY HITTA</u>
By **Misty Holt**
<u>LOVE & CHASIN' PAPER</u>
By **Qay Crockett**
<u>TO DIE IN VAIN</u>
<u>SINS OF A HUSTLA</u>
By **ASAD**
<u>BROOKLYN HUSTLAZ</u>
By **Boogsy Morina**
<u>BROOKLYN ON LOCK I & II</u>
By **Sonovia**
<u>GANGSTA CITY</u>
By **Teddy Duke**
<u>A DRUG KING AND HIS DIAMOND I & II III</u>
<u>A DOPEMAN'S RICHES</u>
<u>HER MAN, MINE'S TOO I, II</u>
<u>CASH MONEY HO'S</u>
By Nicole Goosby
<u>TRAPHOUSE KING **I II & III**</u>

184

KINGPIN KILLAZ I II III

STREET KINGS

PAID IN BLOOD

By **Hood Rich**

LIPSTICK KILLAH **I, II, III**

CRIME OF PASSION I & II

By **Mimi**

STEADY MOBBN' **I, II, III**

By **Marcellus Allen**

WHO SHOT YA **I, II, III**

Renta

GORILLAZ IN THE BAY **I II**

DE'KARI

TRIGGADALE

Elijah R. Freeman

GOD BLESS THE TRAPPERS I, II, III

THESE SCANDALOUS STREETS I, II, III

FEAR MY GANGSTA I, II, III

THESE STREETS DON'T LOVE NOBODY I, II

BURY ME A G I, II, III, IV, V

A GANGSTA'S EMPIRE I, II, III, IV

THE DOPEMAN'S BODYGAURD

Tranay Adams

THE STREETS ARE CALLING

Duquie Wilson

MARRIED TO A BOSS… I II

By Destiny Skai & Chris Green

T.J. Edwards

KINGZ OF THE GAME I II
Playa Ray
SLAUGHTER GANG II
By Willie Slaughter
THE HEART OF A SAVAGE
By Jibril Williams
FUK SHYT
By Blakk Diamond

<u>BOOKS BY LDP'S CEO, CA$H</u>

<u>TRUST IN NO MAN</u>

<u>TRUST IN NO MAN 2</u>

<u>TRUST IN NO MAN 3</u>

<u>BONDED BY BLOOD</u>

<u>SHORTY GOT A THUG</u>

<u>THUGS CRY</u>

<u>THUGS CRY 2</u>

<u>THUGS CRY 3</u>

<u>TRUST NO BITCH</u>

<u>TRUST NO BITCH 2</u>

<u>TRUST NO BITCH 3</u>

<u>TIL MY CASKET DROPS</u>

<u>RESTRAINING ORDER</u>

<u>RESTRAINING ORDER 2</u>

<u>IN LOVE WITH A CONVICT</u>

<u>Coming Soon</u>

BONDED BY BLOOD 2

BOW DOWN TO MY GANGSTA

T.J. Edwards

CPSIA information can be obtained
at www.ICGtesting.com
Printed in the USA
BVHW041012200819
556236BV00011B/804/P

9 781951 081133